Valley
of the
Free

Pandemonium Rising (#0.5)

Michael Sliter

ISBN eBook: 978-0-9998021-4-4
ISBN Print: 978-0-9998021-5-1

Editing by Jennifer Collins
Cover image by René Aigner
Book design and map designs by David O'Meara
Book formatting and interior art by Jeffrey Bardwell

Published by Dragyn Press
DragynPress@gmail.com

Visit http://www.authormikesliter.com/ to sign up for the author newsletter

For Fiona.

Best damn dog friend.

We miss you.

Map of Saiwen (Southern Continent)
and Imsal (Northern Continent)

Legend

Duchy Capital   Country Capital   Country Border

☆   ✿   - - - - - - - - -

TABLE OF CONTENTS

Chapter 1:
Oshwon Valley, Early Summer

Killing a man was easier when he was already dead.

Any life left within him was withering, moaning agony. Each toe had been split and the flesh peeled back, revealing the pale white of bone. His kneecaps had been removed, which seemed like a small thing to a man who'd had his eyes plucked out and his ears torn away. But the knee was more sensitive than both of those, particularly when pierced with wooden nails. His cock had been shorn clear off, too, and lay discarded in the bloodied dirt nearby. The whole mass of dying humanity was ringed by a cloud of flies, some as big as a thumb and all of them fierce biters.

The near-corpse hung by his wrists, knotted ropes forcing his arms apart in a 'v'–perhaps in a mockery of the Yetranian Ascension, the symbol of the goddess whose image was omnipresent across all of Jecusta.

Fortunately, Ferl was not particularly religious. If he had been, maybe his view of the world would have been shattered. Even so, he suppressed a shudder and willed his throat shut to dam any bile from surfacing. He beckoned for two of his men—one of them having been less successful at holding back his cheap breakfast—to cut the ropes that bound the dying man. He thudded into the dirt below, scattering the fog of irate flies for a majestic moment.

Kneeling next to his body, Ferl was thankful that there were no eyes to meet his own as he drove his filigreed dagger into the man's heart.

Had there been eyes, certainly the man would have stared at him with accusation. Probably with hatred, though the he'd always been jovial and affable when alive. But, his hatred would not have been misplaced.

This whole disaster was, after all, Ferl's fault. Though he'd be damned if he'd admit it out loud.

"Stay in groups of five or more. Keep your weapons ready. Watch your steps; the place is littered with traps..." Ferl straightened, not bothering to wipe the blood from his weapon. One of his men started to vomit again, heaving into the heavy foliage just off the barely-beaten path. Ferl ignored him. "Secure a perimeter and start setting up camp. And, for the love of

Ultner's spikey cock, make that screaming stop."

His mercenaries, his newly formed Ferl's Company, set off in all directions, but not without dark looks and bitter muttering. They were a motley lot, but the best that Ferl had been able to round up. He had no reputation and, though his grandfather's inheritance went a long way, it seemed that all of the decent mercenaries already had a home. Or enough common sense to avoid taking on this particular job.

So, he was left with cutthroats, roughs, bully-boys, the odd down-on-his-luck veteran or even worse. Currently, a couple dozen of these soldiers were missing, and their tortured screaming was as omnipresent in the forest as birdsong. Again, Ferl unsuccessfully tried to ignore the piercing, disturbing shrieks. He reminded himself that this was the cost of this business, after all, and it wasn't like any individual ruffian was much of a loss. Half of these men had been condemned to imprisonment or death before Ferl had recruited them anyhow.

Thankfully, not all of his men were useless. There were a couple of reliables, and one pushed past his dispersing soldiers and approached Ferl with a tired salute.

"A poor death," muttered Christoph, one of Ferl's newly-appointed lieutenants. The bearded, swarthy Alganian was twenty years' Ferl's senior, and yet he had no qualms following a younger man.

"I disagree. His death was a mercy. It was the hours leading up to his death that were poor," said Ferl, finally cleaning off his filigreed dagger and turning his back to the remains of the dead man. They wouldn't bury him. Why bother? The roots were too thick in this damnable forest, and they lacked the tools, time, and energy, in any case.

"Semantics, Captain." Christoph procured his favorite accessory, a well-polished cherry pipe. He managed to light it despite the damp, and the scent of *kerena* wafted into the air. Ferl wrinkled his nose at the smell. He'd never been fond of the flavor of the mild hallucinogenic; it reminded him far too much of his grandfather.

"Semantics, dear Christoph, are all we can cling to when the world is falling apart around us. It provides us with order amidst all the chaos. People always seek to *define*—not because the definition matters, but because the process of defining gives us meaning," Ferl replied, gesturing broadly at the forest, lest his own shoulders slump with the effort of optimism.

"You're talking above my head, Captain. Can we just agree that we'd rather he'd not had his cock cut off? Is that sematic enough for you?" Christoph asked with another puff of smoke.

Ferl smirked, though without much mirth. "We can certainly agree that cocklessness is a bad way to go. Now, can we find a dry patch of ground with a bit of distance from this corpse?" Christoph nodded, and fell in next to Ferl as they walked back toward the central knot of mercenaries and relative safety.

His company was busy setting up a rough camp amidst the forest. It was their seventh night here, and they were becoming a little more practiced each time dusk approached. Lean-tos and shelters were tossed about with abandon, wherever the ground was flat or dry enough to allow it. Latrines were being dug and cordoned off, mostly. Tripwires were laid between trees. Cookfires, weak though they were because of the damp, began to heat their meager supply of water to cook piss-poor oatmeal. It was starting to come together. They were rather beginning to look like a real military force.

Ferl flinched as a doughy mercenary caught his foot on a trip wire he'd just laid and pitched, face-first, into the rough root of a tree. Three others nearby burst into laughter, one making a lewd joke punctuated by a thrusting gesture. The fallen man took offense to this, of course. Righting himself, he tackled the offender, the pair rolling through one of the cookfires and spilling boiling water all about, splattering hot liquid on nearby watchers. They, of course, joined in the brawl, which appeared like nothing more than a barfight in the middle of a humid forest.

Ferl sighed. They were fucking doomed.

Ferl had little choice but to ignore the fight and walk away with Christoph. At least it distracted the men from the tortured and the dead, from the awfulness of his poorly-thought out campaign. This valley was not suited to a marching army. Pandemonium's gates, it was hard enough for a pair of men to navigate. The trees were as thick as the hairs on Ferl's head, and the biting insects as omnipresent as lice on the bodies of half of his soldiers. Despite that southern Jecusta was typically temperate, this valley was all sweaty heat, a thick humidity that seemed to cut short breath and fill the throat with the scent of decaying leaves. Ferl mopped at his brow with an already damp sleeve as he strode into what passed as the heart of his camp.

"Ferl..." murmured Ashland, separating herself from the shadow of a tree and moving toward him with the grace of a fairytale goddess. She fell into his embrace almost as if by accident, her lips brushing his cheek. He smiled, but less from her kiss and more at the reminder of Ashland herself.

Maybe they weren't quite doomed.

"My dear, I will never understand how you look as lovely as a magnate's daughter when we are surrounded by such filth," Ferl murmured to her. Christoph snorted and then coughed, but he remained only feet away. He puffed away on his pipe and observed the two of them with a laconic gaze.

Ashland, her night-black hair as wild as she was, tittered in a manner that a magnate's daughter might when the target of flirtation. She rubbed her bare and calloused foot against the back of Ferl's calf.

"And you, blue eyes, are as handsome as a lord." Her voice was deep and heavy, always a little incongruous with her slight build and delicate features. She touched the indent in Ferl's chin, one of her favorite places to rest her thin fingers. Always said it was a good fit.

"All of the lords I've met have been obese bastards who could only find their cocks with help." Ashland arched an eyebrow.

"Well, milord, would you like some help?"

Ferl's smile grew wider. Her hand lingered at his belt; though he'd been with many a woman, despite his young age, Ashland always brought something exciting to his bed. Something intense and unrestrained that called to something deep inside him. Recalling her body, her pure and utter *wildness*, almost made him forgot about the tortured body of his soldier. Almost.

Any passion he felt withered at the thought of a discarded cock laying in the muck. He pushed her away, not unaware of the brief frown that painted her face.

"Later, my dear. For now, we need to plan for tomorrow. Christoph, gather the other lieutenants. In the morning, we make our final march on Oshwona."

Chapter 2:
Farrow's Hold, Late Spring

I can clear out that rat's nest for you," said Ferl, his voice echoing hollowly across the great, draughty hall in the center of Farrow's Hold.

His bold statement was basically ignored as the nobles continued their discussion, quibbling away about the various calamities besetting Jecusta and nibbling on servant-borne delicacies. The Oshwon were the major topic of conversation, as they had just sacked a small town southeast of Farrow's Hold—days away, but still far too close for comfort.

"Why are you here, boy? How did you even get past the guards?" asked a middle-aged, bone-skinny lord, separating himself from a conversation to give Ferl his full attention. Ferl knew him as Rential, a bastard of a man who also happened to be the Magnate of the Low Plains. Ferl supposed that you had permission to be a bastard when you controlled most of the country's grain and corn supplies.

"I am here because I belong here. I am Ferlin Nerial of the Eastern Sweeps. My family—"

Rential snorted. "Your family is an artifact, little more than a bit of mold left over from a bygone era. Honestly, I had thought you all dead."

"Mold, my lord, is very difficult to remove." Ferl puffed his chest with just enough cockiness to be bold without being rude. This court required some level of subtlety, but Ferl didn't have it in him to be overly deferential. It was a character flaw, maybe.

From behind him, Ferl heard a low chuckle. Ferl turned and was greeted by the sight of a middle-aged warrior, a man at least two inches taller and with shoulders twice the size of Ferl's own. Although he was just a touch past his prime, judging from the easy way that the man evaluated him, Ferl saw him as a poor person to cross.

At the warrior's side, of all things, was an Ardian woman. She was older still, and wearing a blue silk dress embroidered with an apple. This woman, Ferl knew. She was the Apple Lady, Escamilla Breen. She had made quite the stir in Ardian politics and was something of a legend, a true rags-to-riches story. Needless to say, Ardian nobility was not enthused by the telling of her story, and nobles were equally likely to scowl as to nod in her direction.

"Ah, Lord Unael. Lady Breen. We are honored that you would join us," Rential said with a skeleton's smile.

"Nonsense. I am honored by the attention of everyone here," Unael replied in a quite unconvincing way. He reached out toward Ferl and shook his hand with the strength of a great ape. The appendage ached by the time the warrior released it, and Ferl had to restrain himself from sticking the aching hand in his armpit.

"Milord, I have heard good things about you and your conquests." Ferl hadn't recognized him at first; he'd expected someone older and even doddering, not someone who could casually crush his hand. The name 'Unael' had been on everyone's lips since Ferl's childhood, so it seemed like he should be ancient. A relic. But, Unael was not that, and judging from the sharpness in his expression, he never would be.

"And I have heard nothing of you. But I have heard that you can 'clear out that rat's nest' for us. Tell me, is that just the talk of overconfident juvenescence?" Unael questioned, looking askance at Escamilla. The angular woman seemed unamused. She had very few smile wrinkles, Ferl noted.

Ferl shook his head. "I am not so young, my lord. And certainly, I have made the best of my twenty years and have experienced things that would make most men shake their heads in disbelief."

Rential rolled his eyes and shook his head, most likely in disbelief. Ferl stood easy with his hands on his hips. He'd not let these men mistake his youth as incompetence. There was that character flaw, again.

Unael's eyes, though, grew cold. "Have you experienced war, my boy? Have you experienced digging your face into the dirt, praying that amidst a barrage of a thousand arrows, you will be the lucky one? Have you experienced driving a sword into the throat of the enemy, only to later realize that he was a person, only following orders just like you? Have you had a friend bleed out at your feet, begging for his life, but with you lacking the skill to hold his lifeblood in? Tell me, have you done any of these things?"

The great hall had quieted, as Unael's deep voice had risen and cut through the droll chatter. Two black cloaks—Jecustan guards—eased through the crowd, hands on their swords in case the newly-minted Lord of Farrow's Hold was in danger from this unknown, blue-eyed boy.

Ferl looked down at his hands. "It wasn't a friend who bled out at my feet. It was my grandfather." Clearing his throat, Ferl met Lord Unael's gaze. "He was killed by the Oshwon."

Now, the great hall was silent, even the servants knowing enough to disappear at such theatrics. There were replaced by more black cloaks who unobtrusively eased into the room. Unael glanced around, seemingly uncertain despite his commanding presence. Escamilla leaned toward him.

"Perhaps we should go elsewhere to discuss this boy's proposal regarding the clearing of the rat's nest?" she suggested in a conversational tone.

"Of course, my lady. Let us retire to my study and discuss the boy's offer." Unael glanced about the room, eyes periodically stopping on clumps of nobles, garishly-dressed and puffed up on their own self-importance. He shook his head slightly.

"Please don't stop your merriment on my account."

***

Unael's study was far less about "studying" and far more about war.

The comfortable, well-lit interior room was lined with weapons of all sorts. There were bows on one wall, including three of the Jecustan yellow yew bows that made their armies infamous, though not necessarily invincible. On another, there were swords of all lengths and makes, ranging from rough-pounded, standard-issue militia blades to the bejeweled swords of kings. Above the fireplace was a great shield that would have been too large for all but the strongest men. Ferl was doubtful that he could even lift the thing.

There wasn't a book to be seen, here, that wasn't about the art of war. Drinso's *Formations of Offense*. Mensk's *The Binding Rules of Combat*. Rance's *Fighting a Greater Enemy*. Ferl recognized nearly every title and had read most of those he knew.

"This place is my retreat," sighed Lord Unael as he draped himself into a padded chair. He released a great sigh. "When I was young, while battling dysentery, I had to defend an undermanned Coralon from the Alganians for three days. We shoved them across six assaults, managing to hold the city until reinforcements arrived. I can't tell you how many times I jabbed my polearm into their masses, and the goddamn thing was *heavy*. And yet, spending one evening with this pack of treacherous nobles is more exhausting than all of that."

Lady Escamilla, who'd found her chair much more gracefully, sat stiff and upright in proper noble form. She placed a hand on Unael's and gave a reassuring squeeze. But her face was cold. Unael cleared his throat upon meeting her frosty eyes.

"But, enough of the struggles of a military man adapting to the world of nobility. I want to know more about you, boy." Ferl was getting a little sick of the moniker "boy," but he held his tongue and kept his face calm and cool. He smiled his most charming smile.

"I am Ferlin Nerial of the Eastern Sweeps. My family—"

"The Nerials? That's a name I haven't heard for a while," Unael interrupted him. "I served under a Samson Nerial in the Fifth for a time, before I had the mishap of being promoted. Out of all of the men I served, I'd say I admired him the most. It's easy to get lost in the politics of the military, but he remained true to his men and to his promises." On Unael's face was a true smile, his eyes deep in remembrance. "Tell me, Ferlin Nerial, is there a relation there?"

"Yes," was all Ferl had to say. He clenched his fists in his lap.

"How is the old bastard? He must be up there in years, but certainly he's earned his retirement."

"Dead, my lord. Like I said, my grandfather

bled out at my feet."

The silence in the room seemed to dim even the candlelight. Ferl said nothing, but instead folded his hands and leaned forward. This was his chance.

"He always spoke highly of you, my lord. He said that you were also true, and that you kept your promises. He said that you made a promise to him, once, long ago. He remembered it, though you had only said it in passing. Do you recall this?"

Unael crinkled his brow and his eyes shifted to one side. He was searching his memory for something from half a lifetime ago. At least half of Ferl's lifetime. And he came up short.

"No, I cannot recall a promise I made to Samson. Though we spoke at times, he was my superior, and there was less of a friendship than a hierarchical respect."

Ferl leaned back in his chair, resting his chin on one hand. "Well, my grandfather was older, and perhaps he was mistaken. But he told me a story of a time when a young soldier, a farm boy, a new recruit, slipped in the muck when marching double-time. He'd been partially trampled by the time grandfather dragged him to his side. This boy—Brox Unael, he said—thanked him profusely, saying, "I pledge myself to you and your family.""

"Yetra's tits, that was your grandfather?"

"My lord, leaders of nations rarely speak of Yetra's tits," Escamilla said in a correcting tone.

"Perhaps they should! The world might be a happier place. Yetra's... I can't believe that was Samson. He'd been wearing a helmet and I was honestly half-dead from the march. My first march, years before I served with him. That was Samson Nerial?" Unael shook his head at the realization.

Ferl smiled authentically at the aging warrior. Despite himself, he liked this man.

Escamilla, though, narrowed her eyes at Ferl. "Rarely does minor nobility think to visit Farrow's Hold without an invitation or agenda. And here you are, Ferlin Nerial, in a meeting far above your station, discussing vague promises made thirty years ago in a moment of weakness. Let us just be clear here. Tell us what you want, or what you think you are owed."

Ferl's smile was frozen on his face. He'd dealt with ladies like this Escamilla before, and he knew what to say. Not that it was an easy thing. "I believe that I am owed nothing. I am just sharing a story. It's what people do when they find they have something in common."

Escamilla was unmoved and Unael shifted back in his seat, seemingly more resistant after Escamilla's words of warning. Damn, Ferl thought, he'd botched this already!

Unael reached behind his chair and fished around for a second until he found a bottle of liquor and three battered iron cups—the type that a soldier might have strapped to their pack while on a march. He filled each cup to the very top with a nearly clear liquid that Ferl didn't recognize; he doubted it was water. Unael pushed cups toward both Ferl and Escamilla. He paused while meeting Escamilla's gaze.

"My lady, I am not so daft that I do not recognize when someone is trying to influence me. Certainly, this boy has a purpose to this journey and to his weak proclamation to help us with the Oshwon. I've little patience for subterfuge and politics, so please spare me this. But, before we talk business, let us have a drink."

Unael raised his cup and Ferl did the same, clanging them together. Escamilla eyed them both, but followed suit with the hint of a smile.

The liquid was like fire down Ferl's throat. He squeezed shut his eyes and grimaced in quite an ugly way as he began to cough and sputter. It wasn't that he wasn't used to strong drink—he'd been downing liquor since he was twelve—but this was simply not palatable. It was practically poison. He set down his cup with shaking hands.

Unael observed with a knowing smile, his own cup missing a mouthful. Escamilla set hers aside without having tasted a drop.

"What in the name of Yetra's cli..." Ferl squinted at Escamilla, biting his tongue. "...is that?"

"The Campaigner's Friend. Cheap to make and cheap to get drunk on. Never could stand the stuff, myself." He took another sip, his face only screwing up a bit. "But, you grow used to something over time and you feel a bit lost without it."

"That's what drunkards say," said Ferl, taking another unfortunate sip from the cup.

Unael sputtered a laugh. "Aye, there's no doubt of that. Now, be straight with me, Ferlin Nerial of the Eastern Sweeps, grandson of Sampson. What is it that you want?"

"I want revenge."

"You say your grandfather was killed by the

Oshwon?" Lady Escamilla asked, skepticism lacing her voice.

"Yes."

"How did it happen?"

Ferl remembered holding his grandfather's body, bloodied and broken.

"I would rather not recall the memory," he said quietly, taking yet another fiery sip. The Campaigner's Friend did seem to be becoming more... friendly. Ferl's body was warm and there was a nice fog in his mind. Everything seemed to lack urgency.

"We all have memories like that, boy," said Unael. He'd already polished off his cup and was in the process of pouring another. "Tell me, what do you know of the Oshwon?"

"Truthfully, I know little. They are in that valley southeast of here, at the convergence of the Low Plains, the Sweeps, and your own territory. It's foreshty," Ferl said, noticing that he was already slurring his words just a bit. He set down the impossibly strong Campaigner's Friend, resolving not to touch it again.

"So, you know a touch of their geography. Congratulations," Escamilla murmured, sitting back in her chair. She, herself, had finally sipped on the drink. Perhaps this was her version of relaxing; only being a touch judgmental instead of a cold bitch.

"The geography tells you nothing of the people. The Oshwon are fiercely independent, so much so that, despite the fact that we bring them nothing but civilization, technology, and ways to make their lives easier, they refuse. They've managed to remain not so much neutral as a no-man's land during Jecusta's own internal wars and natural growth. It has been one of those situations where we don't necessarily need the land, so it's always been safer to just... let them be. It's not worth fighting over a wooded valley when we've plenty of trees."

"But then they left their valley," Escamilla said, perhaps to urge Unael to get to the point. Unael scratched at his budding beard.

"Aye, they left their valley. There'd been word of small things first. Sheep missing, isolated farms looted and burned out. The kind of stuff that could be attributed to any manner of banditry that we deal with even in these days." Ferl raised a brow at that. The more rural parts of Jecusta were famously lawless, particularly since the military was clustered at the borders.

"But it got worsh... Worse," Ferl stated in as controlled a voice as he could muster. He felt himself to be oddly aching for another sip of the Campaigner's Friend. He gave his cup a dirty look.

"It did. You heard, below, of the growing threat from the Oshwon, as if they were horrible foreign invaders bent on our destruction. Truthfully, it is a small thing. Three villages have been burnt out after a party of swords-for-hire were sent into the Oshwon's Valley by an overzealous village council."

"Three villages," began Escamilla, folding her boney hands together in a v-shape, "mean dozens or hundreds of lives. Wherever the fault lies, something needs to be done." Unael gave her a sharp look, and Ferl could feel a tension that might have hunched his shoulders, were he a weaker man.

"I'm very acutely aware of the cost of lives. I used to be infantry, remember? Now, where was I? Ah yes, I cannot mobilize the military for so minor a threat, especially when the Alganians are being particularly aggressive this year, and I cannot pull away from unpredictable Thaul at our southern border. The Ardian border is secure, at least, but we are already spread thin. So, my only option is to employ help to deal with the Oshwon."

"And, I am here, of coursh, to answer your call." Ferl stood up, took the sip he'd promised himself he would not take of the Campaigner's Friend, and gave a goofy bow. He needed to have some of this stuff made.

"You and what Jecustan-sanctioned army?" Escamilla asked, her haughty tone grating at Ferl's dulled nerves. Nonetheless, he spread his arms as wide as his smile.

"Ferl's Company, of course! Have you not heard of us?"

"Of course not. I doubt that anyone has," said Escamilla sharply. He noticed that, though she touched her cup to her lips from time to time, the amount within it remained the same. An old negotiation tactic, that was—appear to be drinking with friends when you were actually quite sober and ready to strike like a cunning old snake. Luckily, Ferl did not need to impress her. Unael was in charge here, ostensibly.

"Well, we are just back on campaign from Sestria, so perhaps we are not as well-known in these parts. But, across the Vissas, we are known as the Scourge of the Sands. The Stealers of

Victory. The Bringersh... Bringers of Mud."

"The Bringers of Mud?" Unael guffawed a little, the alcohol finally cutting through the reservoir of his military stoicism.

"It was raining that day. Now, would you like to hire Ferl's Company to put down the Oshwon? We number over a thousand, trained soldiers all. Should be enough to put down an uprising of fiercely independent but primitive peoples." Ferl, smile still pulling at his lips, sat back down and leaned forward. He was using of all his focus to keeps his words clear and even.

Unael pursed his own lips and crinkled his brow. Escamilla sighed and leaned back, nodding to herself as if some grand theory had been confirmed.

"And you think that Lord Unael would risk his reputation and station by employing some nobody and his imaginary band of warriors? And you are unsanctioned. Only ten sanctioned mercenary companies can operate in Jecusta at any given time, lest they face the wrath of the military," she said, arching an eyebrow.

"The people in this room have the power to make it eleven," said Ferl offhandedly.

Unael shook his head. "We have had other offers, Ferl, from better known—*and sanctioned* —companies. Ultner's Fist, for one. The Ironshod, for another." Ultner's Fist, Ferl had never heard of. But, the Ironshod were near infamous, particularly for their work in the hundred warring states in Thaul. They were called the Tipper of Scales for obvious reasons; they were very much a legitimate mercenary band, and one of the best there was.

"Oh, the Ironshod would certainly be culpab... capable of this job. But, why use a hammer when a dagger would do? More specifically, why pay for a hammer in this case? I can beat their priceshes... prices. Certainly, saving a bit of the national treasury would bode well for a newly-minted lord." Ferl patted his own jingling wallet, fairly full as it was. The room was truly starting to spin.

"Coin is less important to me than results. Frankly, I'd love to lead a force into the valley myself and take the fight to..." Unael trailed off, looking at Escamilla askance. "But that is no longer my role. I've enough to do here. But, I cannot take failure, no matter the cost."

"If you know anything about my grandfather, you will know that failure is not in my blood. You will know that my men are disciplined and trained, so much so that they will never break in the face of the enemy. You will know that I will not rest until our mission is complete. And you will know that I will fight with honor." Ferl nodded, speaking his rehearsed lines with accuracy and not a single slur. He grinned in a manner incongruous to his words.

Unael still looked unconvinced, but at least he did not glance at Escamilla, the bearer of his strings.

"Please, my lord. All I ashk is that you give me the contract. My soldiers aside, let me seek vengeance for my grandfather, the man who you once promised to sherve... serve. I want nothing more than an opportunity; no favors. You need not even sanction us until we are successful."

Escamilla snorted, but Unael just watched

Ferl with unwavering eyes. Considering Ferl's own world was swimming in front of him, it was a pretty impressive feat.

"Fine, Ferl. I will give you this opportunity. We'll discuss pricing—and you *will* beat the others there—tomorrow. But, in four weeks, I expect you to be crossing the border into the valley, a thousand pair of boots marching toward Oshwona, their capital. Within a week from entering their valley, you should have occupied their only real town and crushed any thoughts of future rebellion."

Ferl found himself grinning ear to ear, probably in quite a predatory way. He scaled it back with some effort. "My lord, you will not be dishappointed. Please, can I take my leave? I will have much to do, as my men are currently on leave to celebrate their recent victories. I will have to collect them."

Unael nodded knowingly, smiling as he observed the havoc that the Campaigner's Friend had wrought on the young man.

Ferl pushed himself to his feet, setting down his mysteriously empty cup. The room spun as if he'd rolled down a hill. Ferl tripped on his chair on the way to the door, and only through his immaculate will did he retain his feet. He heard Escamilla saying something ending with the word "mistake," but it was already done. A military man like Unael would never rescind a verbal deal.

Safely out of the study, Ferl leaned against the cold stones of the wall and closed his eyes, waiting for the damnable spinning to stop. Drunk or not, that had gone well. Surprisingly well.

Now, he just needed to find an army.

Chapter 3:
Oshwon Valley, Early Summer

Ferl was terrified. Scared shitless. And useless as a leaking chamber pot.

Trapped in his sleeping sack atop a cheap cot, he could do nothing more than stare up at the Oshwon warrior as the man pushed his way into the modest command tent. He'd knocked over a pack on his way in, waking Ferl in an instant but leaving him as defenseless as if he were still asleep. Where in Ultner's sour anus were his guards? How in Yetra's gaping vagina had this pale, disheveled warrior made his way into the camp through their tripwires and pickets? After the previous night, after the six men were killed in their bedrolls, they'd doubled the guard. Tripled their precautions!

Fuck... fuck, he did not want to die. Fuck this fucking Oshwon bastard, and fuck his Ultner-sucking men.

The Oshwon—a shirtless, flower-tattooed, muscular man—narrowed his eyes at Ferl. The man was pale, even lighter than a Domain dweller, and his dark hair was shorn short. From his leather breeches hung a half-dozen tooth-like knives, and he drew one as he stepped toward Ferl. There was a grim determination on his face.

Ferl tried to leap backwards, but he was well and truly stuck. Damn this sleep sack! It protected the body from huge fucking mosquitos at the cost of any shot at self-defense! He'd die because he'd wanted to avoid a few itchy welts.

"Stop! We'll make a deal! I can make the army turn around! I can help keep your people free!" Ferl shouted, desperation lacing his voice. He thought he might piss himself.

The Oshwon warrior actually paused, tilting his head almost like a dog trying to understand his master. And then, without warning, he pitched forward onto his face. The back of his head was a smoking ruin, and Ashland stepped over his corpse. Her hair was as wild as when she'd left his tent only an hour before.

"Impeccable timing, my dear. How did you know?" Shivering with relief, Ferl finally managed to pull himself from the sleep sack and swing his shaking legs off the side of his cot.

"Know? I just needed another fuck and saw Half-hand and Drench laying in the muck. Well, halves of them, anyhow. They were shorn apart."

"Shorn apart?" Ferl, with trembling hands, began to dress himself. The button on the pants nearly eluded him, but he managed and then buckled the thin sword he favored to his belt. Now that he was awake and starting to calm down, the sweet scent of burning flesh filled his nostrils.

"Shorn. Shredded. Cleaved. This man was a *metsika*."

A *metsika*. A wild mage, one who could draw the life force from either plants, animals, or the earth itself. Was that what they faced? Ferl felt doubly relieved at having survived this attempt.

"Thankfully, my dear, we have you."

Ashland smiled wanly, seemingly distracted. She was always a little off after drawing power, but with her crinkled brows and unfocused eyes, it seemed worse than usual. She glanced down at her bare feet, at the grass that was sneaking around the ill-fitting tarp which formed the floor of his tent. The green was beginning to blacken, curl, and wither. It was...

"Get down!" shouted Ashland, flinging herself at Ferl.

They both impacted the hard ground as the tent exploded around them. Fabric whipped around Ferl's face and the main tent pole slapped into the back of his legs. Abruptly, the early morning sky was visible, and it nearly blinded him while a great whooshing blast shook his ears. He barely knew which way was up, but he felt Ashland push off of him and scrambled out of the mess of destruction.

Ferl at least had the wherewithal to rapidly crawl from the wreckage, though somehow his fucking foot was again tangled in that godsdamned sleep sack! As he tried to yank his foot free, he saw another Oshwon—this one covered in tattoos of tangled vines—grasping at the stem of a blackening bush. There was a frown on his face, and he seemed to be in agony as he turned the foliage to ash. He raised a hand and sent a shapeless blast of green-yellow power at Ferl. Ferl threw his arms across his face, as if the appendages stood a chance at shielding him from certain death.

The power was deflected with a flash, knocked into the camp proper with a small explosion and a chorus of screams.

Ashland had again saved Ferl's life. She had made her way to a tree and was digging her fingers deeply into the rough bark. A cloud of ash began to fall as the leaves wilted and decayed. Without any preamble, she sent her own power— a dozen spinning scythes—back at the tattooed Oshwon. He managed to deflect a couple of them with his own magical shield before being transformed into a mutilated corpse. The nearby trees were splashed with blood and gore.

Nearby, there came the clang of arms as his men battled off more conventional Oshwon forces. Judging from the sounds, Ferl guessed they faced only a handful of attackers rather than an all-out assault, and within moments, the clamor subsided. Likely, the conventional forces were a diversion, giving the Oshwon *metsikas* an honest chance at Ferl's life.

An attempt that had come far too close for comfort.

He extricated himself from the ruins of the

tent, stepped over the severed corpses of Drench and Half-hand, two of his most loyal men, and approached Ashland. She had released the tree; the thing might yet survive. Half the leaves were ash, but the bark seemed hearty and there was still a good deal of green hanging on. She had told him that it took a great deal of effort to fully drain a tree of its lifeforce, and that although she had the ability, she would rather forego killing one completely. She had a soft spot for nature, despite—or perhaps because of—the fact that it was the fuel for her destructive powers.

Ashland's expressive face was painted with fury, staring as she was at the body of the Oshwon *metsika* she'd just killed. Her deep brown eyes were wild, and her fists were clenched so that they were white. Ferl wouldn't have been surprised if she'd rushed the mutilated body and started ripping it to pieces with her bare hands.

Ferl touched her arm gently and she flinched away. He pushed through her resistance, reaching for her again and stroking her arms. She was hurting, right now, and Ferl had always struggled when Ashland was hurting. And, the fact was, he also needed her to be in her right mind if this venture still stood a chance. He spoke to her with a soft voice.

"My dear, you should get some rest. Now that the sun rises, we should have some time to make order out of this attack and prepare for the final push to Oshwona. We'll of course need you more than anyone."

Ashland closed her eyes and inhaled deeply, holding onto the air as if it was her last breath.

After a long minute, or maybe two, she released it with deliberation.

"Did you see those men? Those Oshwon *metsikas*?" Her voice was quiet, considering.

"I didn't get a good look; I was a little distracted by their knives and their fucking beams of power. And..." Ferl repressed a shudder as he glanced at the shredded pile of flesh laying amidst the ash nearby, "now there's isn't much to look at."

"They did not want to fight. They did not want to draw—his face was pained as he pulled *yenas* from that bush. There were *tears* in his eyes."

"So? He probably realized that you were about to blast him into oblivion," Ferl said with a smirk. Unamused, Ashland turned her back to him. Ferl started after her, unsure exactly how he'd pissed her off, but he was interrupted by some approaching soldiers.

"Captain!" Lieutenant Christoph ran up with a couple of sergeants in tow. Ferl squinted. Paran, the bearded, hairless, supposedly-veteran bastard was one of them. Ferl didn't like him, but he liked his results; Paran was utterly ruthless, and perfect for keeping the undisciplined mob in line. The other, Dammey, had too soft a touch and was probably unsuited to both leadership and mercenary work. But, the men were fond of him, and that was enough to keep them moving in the right direction. Truth be told, Ferl liked his quick smile and his sense of honor.

But now was not the time for smiles or honor.

"What in the fuck happened here, Christoph? What happened to our perimeter? Do our men *want* to die?" The lieutenant's face was fearful, and it was not because of Ferl's words. There was blood on his hands, and he wiped them on his shirt to little effect.

"Sir, they were here *before* we camped. They know this land, every hole and every crevice, and they waited until we let our guard down."

"The fuckers..." growled Paran. He scratched at his gnarled beard. "There weren't many, but they got a bunch of us while we were sleeping. Right in the throat with those tooth knives." He poked Dammey in the neck, though the man batted his hand away. Paran poked him again and Dammey smacked his wrist with a snarl. He shouldered Paran to the side.

"Captain, several of the Oshwon managed to escape with prisoners. They used some poisonous fog to render men unconscious. I expect... I expect we will be hearing their screams shortly."

More soldiers were becoming visible in the early morning fog. Some were in mismatched leather armor while others were still in their underclothes. A few were bloodied, and all held weapons, glancing about the forest nervously as if the trees themselves might leap out and grab them. Ferl sighed and painted on a false smile, searching for his charisma somewhere amidst the fear and uncertainty.

"No worries, Sergeant. This will be over soon. No more nights in this Ultner-fucked place..." Dammey, though usually affable, did not look convinced. Rather, he had the wild eyes of a child who feared the monster under his bed.

Ferl continued. "Christoph, get the men sorted. Leave our camp as-is so we can steal a march on them. Their pitiable capital is close..."

"We ain't marching no more!" shouted one of the soldiers, a gap-toothed Sestrian with a thick accent. He held up his spear threateningly, and a couple more men did, too. "You're just sending us to our deaths!"

"And what the fuck do you think it means to be a mercenary?" Paran spat, making the recalcitrant soldiers flinch.

"It means fighting on a battlefield, not being whittled down two-by-two and having our cocks cut off before they gouge out our eyes! Not having fucking magical blades cut us in half!" shouted another soldier, kicking dirt at one of the sliced-up dead men. This one who'd spoken up was a horse of a man, bigger than anyone had the right to be. He was a clumsy fuck and would likely be slaughtered in an honest battle, but Ultner be damned if people weren't terrified of him. And, people tended to rally behind what frightened them.

The crowd was growing a backbone.

Ferl slapped at a big fucking mosquito and found that his palms were sweating. More soldiers were pointing their spears at him; it was a firmly unsettling experience. He turned in a circle, speaking to no one in particular but finding that moving helped him stay calm.

"You would think to mutiny? Now? When we are so close to our destination?" Happily, his voice had not fluttered.

Sergeant Dammey turned toward Ferl, his face messed up with grief, guilt, and shame barely covered by a veneer of determination. He drew his sword but kept the point down. "Sorry, Captain. I think it's time that we turn around.

The men have lost their heart for this. It's been too much, no matter what the pay."

Ferl eyed Dammey's sword and then read his face. Would the man actually strike? Did he have the guts for it? It seemed unlikely, but Ferl had learned to always take a man with a sword seriously.

"Well, we still want the pay!" shouted the giant soldier. A few chuckled nearby, not with much enthusiasm. But, their spears were still leveled at his heart. Where the fuck was Ashland?

Ferl shook his head and pointed a firm, accusatory finger at the big soldier. "You shit-covered coward. I keep my money in a bank, not up my asshole like the rest of you. You mutiny, you get nothing. In fact, you get the *reputation* of mutineers, assuming the Jecustan military doesn't decide to imprison or kill you on the spot. And I own half of your criminal writs—if you're found walking around without that, you're doomed. We have a *contract*, boys. And the contract says that we will do this thing, unpleasant though it may be."

"We ain't too far from Thaul. Mercenaries are always welcome in the warring cities!" shouted the first soldier, the gap-toothed instigator.

"Sure. Mercenaries. Not a band of cutthroat criminals without a victory to their name or an ounce of fighting spirit. They are called the warring cities because *they make war*. They don't tuck tail and run like a bunch of motherless scum-pickers." Ferl was gaining confidence. "And do you know what would happen if you did try a retreat through this gods-forsaken valley? You would turn your back on an enemy, a dangerous enemy who would have found strength in your weakness. A quarter of you would end up left behind and spitted by the Oshwon. Your screams would be the Oshwon's cry of defiance to the world. These men seek their independence, and only through your pain will that be true."

The wall of spears was beginning to drop. The spine of the crowd was beginning to bend. All Ferl needed to do was slam it against his knee.

"You're scared. You should be. This is terrifying shit that we do. But, would you rather kill or die? Because that is your option! Follow me, and we will crush the Oshwon. Today. Leave me, kill me—whatever you decide to do—and either you or a friend will die, if not both. Oh, and you need not even wait for the Oshwon. See that shredded bit of flesh over there? See that bit of brain hanging from those low branches? That is what Ashland will do to every... last... fucking... one of you."

Ferl was breathing heavy now with the passion of his words, with the excitement coupled with the fear of death. He'd never truly fought in a battle before and had no desire to do so, but this—controlling men through persuasive fear or igniting their pride—*this* was his type of battle.

The men were coming around, digging the points of their spears into the ground. Even the gap-toothed Sestrian and the horse-sized monster of a soldier let loose their weapons, faces either shamed or resigned. They'd all feel better when they were paid, assuming they survived.

Ferl had won, but he needed to make sure that this didn't happen again.

"Ferl's Company, get dressed and armed, and

then report to your immediate superiors. I will forgive your fear this one time. But I cannot tolerate insubordination from my own command."

Dammey was not prepared as Ferl's dagger whipped up and entered his mouth through the soft spot beneath his chin. His eyes—the strike had not killed him immediately—were wide and wet with pain, and his arms batted softly at Ferl's. His threatening sword had fallen to the ground with a damp thud.

This was much harder than killing a near-dead torture victim.

Ferl had never killed a good man before. It was... something else. It didn't feel good. But Ferl supposed that he would get used to it, in this line of work.

He withdrew the blade and Dammey fell to the ground. Ferl knelt down and finished the job, then looking up at his men and steeling his expression.

"Well, did I say we are going to stand around? Make ready! Today, we kill the Oshwon."

And a single, high-pitched and tortured scream cut through the valley like the call of a hawk.

Chapter 4:
Fort Aurabourne, Late Spring

I can do better. Fifty yets a head for their writs, and they come with me."

The sailor, a shipwreck of a man, shook his head. "Nah, they're all convicted criminals. The magnate has 'is orders, and I'm just following 'em."

Ferl stepped back and wiped his forehead with the back of his arm. It was fucking humid in Fort Aurabourne, and the breeze from Lake Seens did little to lessen the everlasting perspiration that was saturating Ferl's lengthening hair. He did need a haircut, but lacked the time.

The docks weren't exactly expansive, limited as they were by the rocky geography of the coast. They were rotting, filthy, and choked with dirty laborers and sopping sailors. But the congestion actually helped Ferl narrow his search. Aside from an army of fishermen, the only people coming through Fort Aurabourne were soldiers, criminals, and prisoners of war. His plan was to take any and all of them for his budding Ferl's Company.

He sighed and placed a hand on the sailor's bare, sunbeaten shoulder. "Listen, friend. I get that Magnate Linstael has his orders. 'Prisoners are to be locked up in the fort until their sentencing, whereupon they will be distributed across Jecusta to serve in labor camps or, if they are not convicted of violent crimes, servants.' It makes sense. Really, it does."

Ferl turned away. "But the labor camps are full right now. The Alganian war prisoners are thick in those places, almost so that it is more of a vacation because there is little enough work to go around! And, my friend, do you know what will happen if there is nowhere for these criminals to go? They stay in the fort. They might even be released into the town on bond. Tell me, do you have a family?"

The grizzled, battered man nodded his head. "Aye, a wife and two girls, newly grown."

Hopefully taking after their mother in looks, Ferl thought. But, he maintained his affable smile. "And would you want these men around your girls?" Ferl pressed. "Your wife? Absolutely not. Give me their writs and I will do you the double service of taking them off your hands and paying near twice as much as you'd get from the magnate. He'd certainly forgive you for it. Or even thank you. Besides..." Ferl leaned forward conspiratorially, "my company marches for Unael. Half of the criminals will likely end up dead. You'd be doing the entire country a favor."

The sailor narrowed his eyes at Ferl and stared with the gaze of someone who often focused on the horizon. And then he smirked shrewdly. "Sixty yets per head, and I need assurances that they are being recruited for this *sanctioned* mercenary company of yours. Hard documents, mind you, notarized by a banker and citing Unael's name."

Ferl grinned. He'd found himself an entrepreneur. "Oh, suddenly your grammar has improved, my friend. How long have you been playing at sailor?"

"A sailor is what I am and have always been, but I'm not an idiot. You people tend to think we're simple because of how baked our skin is; the brains beneath are preserved by the salt of the water."

Ferl shrugged, not willing to point out that Lake Seens was a freshwater lake, nor that this man was indeed an idiot. He'd have been willing to pay seventy-five yets a head.

"You are right, my friend," Ferl told him. "After meeting you, I will not underestimate a person like you again."

They grasped each other's wrists and exchanged money, writs, and directions on delivering the criminals to Ferl's makeshift camp south of the fort.

That brought his force up to nearly five

hundred. Almost halfway there, and only about a week until he forced a march to the Oshwon Valley. He was going to be thoroughly fucked unless he managed some miracle. Maybe five hundred deserters would decide to join up with him in exchange for protecting their identities. Or, perhaps a band of pirates, landlocked and far from home, would raise the banner of Ferl's Company as a symbol of hope. Most likely, though, he'd manage to drudge up a couple hundred more scumbags and lead them all to a near certain slaughter at the hands of the Oshwon.

At which point he'd sneak away and find a new life in Thaul, or maybe sail north across the Vissas to Sestria. He'd often lied about seeing that land; perhaps he should learn more about Sestria in order to actually offer a kernel of truth to his stories. He had the money for years of lavish living and relaxing travel, after all.

Of course, lavish living wasn't the goal of starting up his company.

He began walking back through the town, trying to plan out his next move. He'd emptied this place of criminals and started to intercept such prisoners before they ever reached their destination. But, this was an unpredictable plan, and he'd no idea whether more would come through in the next week. Ferl had had an informant that fed him intelligence about new arrivals and potential recruits, but the informant himself had now been imprisoned for going on a murdering spree after someone had pointed out that he was bald. Black Jack had always been a bit odd.

Thankfully, Jecustan law did allow for criminals to be purchased as indentured soldiers in government-sanctioned mercenary forces, and Ferl did have a contract from Unael explicitly naming Ferl's Company as a candidate for sanctioning. So, he had credibility if not reputation. Even so, invoking Unael's name only drove up the price, so he tried to keep that a secret. He'd rather hang onto as many yets as possible as he strove to start this venture. He never knew when he'd have to cut and run, after all.

The confines of the streets of Fort Aurabourne were even more stifling than the docks. The stink of fish combined with the pungent odor of horse leavings, sweating bodies, and poor sanitation practices was a pure achievement that only humanity could boast. Squeezing between two overweight fish mongers, Ferl wondered if anything else in the animal kingdom was as disgusting as humanity was. He had sincere doubts.

With a week left, he'd have to move quickly and make some bold moves. Eying some uncomfortable, sweating Aurabourner guards as they passed, he wondered whether he could bribe any away from this filth with the lure of money and a pinch of glory. He'd have to emphasize the money bit, as the glory was dubious at best. He'd read that the best companies never had to draw a blade, and that was the approach he'd like to go with. At the very least, he'd personally like to never come within striking range of an enemy's weapon. Again, he'd read that the best commanders never had to actually fight. It was the very poor commanders who either led the charge or let the enemy break through the lines to reach them.

Ferl glanced about the congested town looking for landmarks. His next goal was to find a veterans' guild hall, or at least the bar where veterans tended to get drunk and relive their glory days. Having some experience would be good for his forces, and every once in a while, you might find a true fighter mixed in with all of the amputees and washouts.

Although, finding anything in this Ultner-maze-fucked town would take half the day.

"I hear you are looking for bodies," said a voice from just over his shoulder. To Ferl's credit, he barely flinched even as his hand darted to the thin sword at his waist. He pivoted and stepped back, taking in the woman who had whispered in his ear.

She was middle-aged, but in a flattering way. She could have been his mother's age, assuming his mother was still out there somewhere. With honey eyes and manicured, made-up features, it was obvious that this was no sailor's wife or fishmonger, and nor did her features appear to be used to hard labor. She stood out amidst the crowd, and it was clear that she had no intent to blend in. All in all, she was quite a lovely creature.

"You make me sound like a crypt-keeper." Ferl smirked cautiously, observing this strange, out-of-place woman.

"I would have said 'soldiers,' but your methods seem to be less focused on that aspect of recruiting a mercenary force." The woman's tone was flat, her face impassive.

"Any hand can be trained to wield a sword," Ferl said, holding his own hands up as if to say 'I'm certainly trained, so watch yourself.'

The woman said nothing. The two stood considering each other in the middle of the busy, muddy throughway, but the crowd seemed to part around them, creating a sort of pseudo privacy. Eventually, Ferl shrugged. "Okay, you obviously didn't come here to small-talk. You've come to make me a sort of offer. Will you tell me what it is?" The woman folded her hands in front of her, and he noticed they were encrusted with rings that were likely valued at more than this entire town.

"I will. But not here. I find the smell rather off-putting."

"In that, you and I agree, lady. Fine, take me to your sinister den or wherever you do your back-alley dealings. I'd like to have this done by dinner, as I have a date I would rather not miss."

The woman cracked a small smile for the first time. It seemed to be an unfamiliar expression on her face and didn't fit the coldness reflected by her eyes.

"Then follow me to my sinister den."

Ferl grinned in return as she pivoted and began to walk toward the fort proper.

Maybe this woman was, in fact, the miracle he'd been hoping for.

**

If Ferl had had a den of his own, he would have modeled it after this one.

Comfortable was a word for it. Lavish would be more accurate. Opulence might be pushing it, but only just barely.

In the literal shadow of Fort Aurabourne, this place was camouflaged as a boarding house but was in reality a mansion. All around Ferl were signs of excess. Scantily silk-clad women of all races floated about, tending to the needs of the people seated within the massive, bright chamber. As he watched, a slender Rafónese woman—barely more than a girl—oiled up her hands and began to rub the shoulders of a shirtless and undoubtedly overweight Jecustan noble. With all the tension he was feeling right now, Ferl would not have been opposed to that same treatment himself.

The scent of the grand chamber was a fine perfume coupled with the mouth-watering hint of a wood grill from a nearby kitchen. He detected the aroma of roasting pork and chicken—the Jecustans did not prefer light delicacies—that was thankfully without any fish to crinkle his nose. He would always rather avoid food from the sea, which made Fort Aurabourne all the more loathsome. Nobles and other well-dressed patrons tore into their meals, washing them down with fine Sestrian wine. Ferl recognized some of the labels, and therefore knew these patrons must be rich.

Even through the perfume and food, *kerena* wafted through the halls, the slight hallucinogenic amplifying the pleasure of the patrons.

He lounged on an overstuffed chair, sitting across from the woman who had so subtly approached him in the street. She had spoken little as they'd muscled their way through the crowd, but at least provided a name. Violet, she called herself. As false a name as any he'd heard, but that was fine. He was not opposed to a false title or two himself.

"So, what do you think of my dark and sinister headquarters? The place from which I run my evil empire?" Violet asked, arching a perfectly manicured eyebrow.

"I was just thinking I'd love to get myself one of these," Ferl murmured, his eyes still on the Rafónese woman. He'd never been with a girl from across the Vissas Sea before, though he'd heard flattering rumors.

"It takes a good deal of hard and honest work." Violet leaned back in her own chair and reached to the side without looking. Almost as if by instinct, a serving girl placed a glass of wine in her hand and glided off without a sound.

Ferl tried the same, but found his hand empty. Violet, crossing her legs in front of him, smiled for the second time in a way that was not matched by her eyes. "They don't know you. They don't know your habits. And I haven't decided whether to kill you yet."

Ferl hid the quick shiver that covered his arms in goosepimples behind a forced smile. He was suddenly quite aware that the room was ringed in blank-eyed guards, all of them dressed in leathers dyed the color of their mistress' name.

"I hadn't realized that my life was on the table," Ferl said glibly. He started mapping out an escape route. Windows were too high. Doors were too guarded. If it came to blows, he was as fucked as a Yetranian Taneo in a gambling house.

"Come now. You are young and handsome,

but anytime you are invited, alone and disarmed, into the home of someone who is likely a criminal, there's a good amount of danger involved. Secrets are not revealed cheaply, and I need to trust you. If I don't, you're dead. But... no worries. If it comes to that, I will allow you a glass of wine first. It's just good manners." Violet's face was passive, her voice deadpan. Ferl had no doubt she'd follow through on her threats.

"So, you need trust. Young though I am, I know that means money."

"Handsome *and* smart." Violet said nothing more, simply observing Ferl with the fixed look of a predator.

Though he felt like a bear at a circus sideshow, Ferl resisted moving or fidgeting. His mentor had taught him that confidence was ten percent internal and ninety percent body language. Though, internally, he felt a sudden desperation to flee, fully knowing he'd be cut down, he forced himself to relax and sit easily in his chair. His legs were crossed, his hands resting comfortably on the armrests. He met her honey gaze with his own blues, these being the same eyes—along with a clever tongue—that had seduced many unsuspecting women. Violet was not quite so easily swayed, however.

Eventually satisfied with whatever she was searching for, she waggled her fingers, and Ferl found that a glass of wine appeared in his hands so suddenly that he nearly dropped it.

"Well, shall we talk business?" Violet asked, setting down her own glass. She was still so impassive; her face seemed fairly unfamiliar with the expression of emotion.

"I suppose we should. How, precisely, could you help me? What is it that you do, here?"

Violet tutted, wagging a finger at him. "You'll learn as much as you need to. But, needless to say, I have an abundance of men right now who might be of service to you." In the corner of the chamber, a harpist began to play an entrancing tune. Ferl recognized the first chords of a classic song. If one walked into a tavern on a weekend, odds were good that one would hear some rendition of "The Desperate Wanderer." It was a near endless song outlining the journeys of Eramore, the Jecustan knight who searched ceaselessly for his stolen wife, Raslin. He'd supposedly been on a hundred adventures in search of her, and "The Desperate Wanderer" continued to grow with his legend. It was impossible to tell the truth from the fantasy, as the stories continued to change. Ferl hated "The Desperate Wanderer" with a passion.

A clear, clarion male voice emanated from a handsome Jecustan boy; it was a voice that belied his small stature and weak frame. He began the story at the beginning, when Lady Raslin was taken by the Band of the Crimson Blades. Ferl set his jaw against the tune and found himself having to speak louder to be heard. "Okay. I can pay for these soldiers—what is the cost to hire your men for an immediate job? How many do you have?"

Violet didn't seem to raise her voice, and yet Ferl could still hear her easily. "It's not a hire or not hire situation. I would say it is more of a purchase."

"A purchase? I don't understand the distinction." Playing coy, Ferl sipped on his wine, the Sestrian vintage as delightful as he'd expected. It was full-bodied with hints of herbs, the currant undertones betraying the youth of this particular bottle. But Ferl had always thought that newer wine was better than old; he'd often enough lost arguments in that direction.

Violet set down her own glass on the table between them. "I think that you do, smart and handsome boy."

And Ferl did. Slavery had been made illegal in Jecusta thirty years ago, coming with the sweeping changes made by a new generation of magnates, the regional rulers of the country. Frankly, none of them were particularly progressive, but there'd been enough political pressures from their Ardian and Thaulish allies to abolish the outdated practice.

Most Jecustan slaves had been born to the lifestyle, sentenced to it, or made captive from various wars. When it had been abolished, owners—mostly plantation owners, city nobles, and the government in general—had been forced to provide emancipation papers, private owners being subsidized by the Jecustan Council. Then, the former owners had been forced to pay livable wages—barely so—in order to allow these freed people a chance to have a real life.

When the former masters had resisted and sent their previous slaves packing, many had joined the military. A good deal of them had fought, and been killed, in the constant border skirmishes with Algania. But, as Lord Unael had come to power over the past twenty years, he'd been universally supported by soldiers and former slaves alike—granting him broad, sweeping appeal.

Meanwhile, much of Jecusta's extensive farmland had been left untended and returned to weed and wild. Starvation periodically plagued the country, magnified by the seven-year drought. In bigger cities, buildings once maintained by slave labor had begun to fall into disrepair. Farrow's Hold, for instance, was known to be a shadow of itself.

Much of this, of course, had happened before Ferl had been born. Slavery was just something that old people grumbled about when they reminisced about "better days." Of course, Farrow's Hold had looked better, years ago. Of course, they'd used to eat better, years ago. So on and so forth. The ramblings of men whose best years were behind them.

Even so, Ferl had heard that slavery still flourished in pockets in Jecusta. An illegal practice, certainly, but corruption was not exactly unknown in more backwater provinces. Like Fort Aurabourne, it seemed.

"You are offering me slaves," Ferl said bluntly. He observed the beautiful Rafónese woman as she sensually rubbed the back of the overweight man. The feel of the place shifted, and he noticed her smile was much more forced than he'd noted previously. He saw that the guards' impassive faces were tight with clenched jaws. He observed the patronage's casual neglect of the girls as they walked around—slapping, insulting, or just ignoring them. Each serving person wore a violet bracelet, too... less a mark of employment and more one of ownership. Most everyone here must be a slave, Ferl realized.

Meanwhile, the harpist continued Eramore's tune, and the words of the boy echoed throughout the chamber like a closing noose. They both wore violet bracelets, as well.

"Once you've paid, they are yours. You can do whatever you please with them. Three hundred and forty men to bolster your forces."

Ferl paused, his wine glass inches from his mouth. That would give him almost what he needed. He could fill in the rest of his ranks with veterans, but he'd be able to march to the Valley of the Oshwon within days, actually meeting Unael's demand.

"Three hundred and forty slaves, who, by definition, are held against their will. And you think it would be a good idea for me to equip them with sharp objects and march them toward death? What would you expect the outcome to be?"

"Every piece of merchandise I offer is well broken in, I assure you. There will be no worries about disobedience, Ferl of Ferl's Company. And there are methods to ensure their loyalty. They'll be more trustworthy than the rest of the cutthroats you've recruited so far."

As Violet stared at him with her honey eyes, Ferl's stomach began to tingle, almost imperceptibly. It was as if a handful of ants had taken up residence in the organ and were dancing about as they sought to find an escape. His hand darted to his belly, and then his eyes rested on the glass of wine. His hands began to shake. *Poison.*

"What did you do me?" Ferl realized his breath was coming in gasps. Violet's face was yet impassive.

"This is what we call the Liquid Collar. It is a mild poison that can, over time, burn the lining of the stomach and infect the body. The slaves each have a dose with dinner every third day, and then they are given the antidote, mixed with the next dose, three days later. It is a delicate balance, to poison while healing, but my herbologists have perfected it. The slaves' stomachs always feel like yours—a reminder, if you will—but they rarely experience overt pain. They've little motivation to run when they would surely be dead within a month."

Ferl closed his eyes on focused on his breathing. If she'd wanted him dead, he would be dead by now. *Ninety percent body language.* He removed his hand from his stomach and calmly steepled his fingers.

"Are you planning on keeping me as a slave, then? People would notice if I went missing, you know."

Violet nodded quite matter-of-factly. "Of course not. I would not risk making a free man into a slave. Mine are all taken in the traditional ways."

"Then, do you poison all of your guests?"

"Around half." She again waved her hand, and this time one of the violet-armored guards appeared at her side bearing a small vial with a green substance inside. "Two drops, under your tongue. You will feel better within the hour."

Hurriedly, Ferl followed the instructions, only realizing afterward that it might have been a different type of poison he'd ingested.

Lesson learned; don't trust food or drink from

attractive slave owners.

It may have been his imagination, but it already felt like the figurative ants were dying off in his stomach. He exhaled slowly, releasing the tension of the moment.

"If I were to take your slaves, Violet, this seems like a lot of extra management."

"I would provide you with a cook, a woman skilled in balancing the Liquid Collar. You would keep this force separate from the others and it would be fine," she answered, glancing around as if she were bored of the conversation.

"Again, it seems like a hassle, and I'm not sure..."

Violet turned back to him, a line forming between her narrowed eyes. "I've already spent enough time with you, Ferl. You want to be a fucking mercenary captain. You have a destination in mind and need an army. If you worry about the hassle of our arrangement, use basic tactics. *The slaves die first*. No one to worry about feeding then."

Ferl almost shrank away from her anger. This was one cold bitch, but what she said made sense. Ferl would have to get used to sending men to their deaths, after all, given this course he'd committed himself to. Ferl inclined his head, tacitly agreeing to the deal.

Violet rose, nodded to him, and called over a man who, from his ink-stained hands, was a scribe or a contract-writer. Ferl had one more question, though, burning his tongue.

"What's to stop them from killing this cook of yours, curing themselves, and then chopping the rest of us to bits?"

"Like I said, my men are sufficiently broken and the Liquid Collar has a delicate balance. Take too much or too little, you die. But, just in case..." Violet rubbed two fingers together. "I will need payment up front."

Chapter 5:
Oshwon Valley, Early Summer

Rennid watched warily as Ferl approached his campfire. The boy-captain's irritatingly handsome features appeared grim for a change. The arrogance was washed away, perhaps because so many had died and his men had nearly revolted. Or perhaps because he had been forced to kill. It was a sad thing, the loss of confidence and youth.

But none of that mattered to Rennid, for Rennid was a slave—and he cared as little for Ferl as he had for Violet or any previous master. He was loathe to empathize with any master, though at least this Ferl was better than most. He gave them as much autonomy as a marching army would allow, and he did not have them beaten. In fact, when one of his other soldiers—convicts, almost to a man—had backhanded Rennid for speaking out of turn, Ferl had the solider tied to a tree and had *him* lashed.

That criminal-soldier had fallen behind and been taken by the Oshwon, itself as bad a punishment as any. Rennid had smiled darkly at his screams.

"Sergeant Rennid." Ferl nodded to him. He looked tired, the boy-captain did. And Rennid stayed alive by noticing the details, like the blood staining the hilt of Ferl's dagger. Someone had recently died to his blade. The whispers were that it had been Sergeant Dammey, but Rennid had kept himself and his slave-soldiers well away from that little mutiny. Ignorance was often much safer than knowledge in a case like this. In most cases, really.

"Captain." Rennid spoke minimally. He was always sparse in his communication. His parents had taught him as much before they'd been sold and separated. You say less, you attract less attention. Less attention means less danger, of course. Less likelihood of being beaten or worse.

Ferl eyed him, perhaps searching for a sign of disobedience. Rennid did not flinch and he kept his eyes carefully lowered, fixed on the small dimple in Ferl's chin. Lower the eyes too much and, as with a submissive dog, the temptation to strike might be too much. It was a balance, being subservient, an act as fine as any required by a player. Not that Rennid attended many plays, but Violet occasionally had actors brought in for her patrons. Rennid was better than all of them.

"I need you to gather your men and make ready. We are taking this fight to the Oshwon. We will split up our forces into three groups. You, my friend, will lead your men from the west, right into the center of their town. The other two groups will come from the north and south, allowing you to cut right into the heart of Oshwona. I expect that they will yield with little effort when confronted with a frontal assault."

"Yes, Captain." Obviously a suicide mission, rushing into the center of the only real city of that the Oshwon could claim. Rennid was not so stupid as to think otherwise. But, his life had basically been made a battle with death, given the damnable Liquid Collar dancing in his stomach. Ferl nodded and almost started away, but then he paused for a long moment and bowed his head. He turned back to the slave-sergeant.

"Oh, and when we survive this, I will gift you all the cure. You will be welcome to follow me for the same pay as the rest of the men, but you will no longer be compelled. I have felt the tickle of the Collar; I've little motivation to expose other men to that same feeling." Rennid noticed that Ferl's hands were twitching. It was a lie, certainly. A sweet lie, though, and one that instilled him with a damnable, bleeding false hope. Nefora be burned if he didn't still love the taste of hope, despite the fact that the promise was as wispy as the vines hanging above them.

"Yes, Captain." Rennid nodded. It wouldn't take long to gather his men. They were the poorest equipped, after all. Few had armor and most wielded clumsy spears—the kind that a farmer might use to prod a wandering wild pig off his property. It'd likely not be enough. They'd likely all die.

Of course, he would not tell his men that. He'd give them some measure of hope. But he'd also not tell them of Ferl's false promise.

He'd rather horde that lie for himself.

***

Ferl's face spasmed into a frown as he watched the stocky Alganian slave march off toward his compatriots—the third of his army who were not motivated by money, but rather compelled by poison and broken by a lifetime of obedience. And yet, a fiery rebellion burned in Rennid's marble grey eyes. The man thought he hid it, but it was there, clear to see.

But Rennid would never act on his urge to run away. It was not loyalty or fear that drove his compliance, but rather an incredibly strong sense of self-preservation. Slaves were the strongest of all of them, to persist through such straights, to thrive on neglect. They were more persevering than the hungriest of wolves, more resilient than arctic bears. For they fought to stay alive every single day of their existence with no hope for a better life.

Ferl wondered if it was cruel for him to dangle hope in front of Rennid like a fisherman would dangle bait. Would it help the man fight harder? Would it inspire his slave-soldiers to choke the path with their bodies in case the survivors might be freed?

He meant it, though, Ferl did. He would free these slaves and give them whatever they wished. He'd no wish to risk being known as a slaver or to maintain this poison-cure-poison cycle. It would certainly be a hassle, anyhow, as Violet had admitted.

The poorly-equipped slave army was already nearly assembled as he watched. They'd picked up their spears and begun to form loose ranks with the discipline of those who always followed orders. It wouldn't be long until their cheap spears ran red with blood. Or until they were left broken in twain, scattered among the bodies of their owners.

Ferl needed to find Ashland, but he struggled to turn away from Rennid and his men. Unconsciously, Ferl's lips turned down again as Violet's words echoed in his mind.

The slaves die first.

Chapter 6:
Fort Aurabourne, Late Spring

There were always some places that shunned newcomers, particularly those who were young, handsome, and whole.

One such place was this so-called Veterans Hall One Hundred and Twenty-Six, a number as meaningless as the lives of most who occupied the run-down old shack in Fort Aurabourne. Soldiers certainly washed out of the military at young ages, in their late twenties after getting their silver ten-year chit. And yet, the occupants of this place tended to be a bit more... corpse-esque in nature.

Ferl groaned as he pushed open the creaky

doors and glanced around the common area, seeing far less than he'd hoped for. He immediately became the target of fifty red-eyed glares.

"What da fuck you doing here, boy? You ain't no veteran," spat a giant, prickly-bearded man. Though his arms were the size of small tree trunks and still rippled with muscle, most of his girth has shifted to his gut. As the man struggled to his feet, Ferl could think of nothing more than a turtle struggling to roll over.

Ferl nodded with as much politeness as he could muster. "No sir, I am not a veteran. But, I am an admirer." He regretted his choice of words immediately.

"An admirer, eh? You admire this?" Another man—a broken-down, one-legged amputee—pulled up his shirt, revealing a carpet of hair and a surprisingly brown nipple. The crowd laughed bawdily and old former soldiers clinked crocks together, seemingly unaware that their ale sloshed over onto the sticky floor, continuing to transform the entire place into a beehive.

Ferl waited a moment for things to settle.

"Doubtful that anyone has ever swooned over you, sir. But, regardless, what I do admire is what you have done for our country. That you have protected our people. That, in our time of..."

"Horseshit, pretty boy." This from a wire of a man, probably the youngest in the room. The irony was that he was fairly handsome himself. Maybe he was the love-soldier, the type the others kept around for their evening pursuits. Ferl'd heard tell of such things, and the man's androgynous features, as well as the way others leered at him, would be consistent with that.

"I am offended that you doubt my words," said Ferl with a small frown. The crowd hooted, hollered, and hissed at him. Drunken sops. This was a lost cause. Ferl shook his head and turned to leave.

The first one who spoke up, Prickly Beard, shouted out, "Boy, give us yer piece. We ain't unfamiliar with the wandering merchant. Some o' these fools might want to buy what yer sellin'. You've one minute." He waved back the crowd of veterans in their various states of inebriation and they quieted fairly quickly.

Ferl sighed deeply, his heart not truly in the pitch. Criminals, slaves, and now this rabble. But he turned back to them. "My fellow Jecustans, I come to you not with things to sell, but with a proposition."

"I bet you do," sneered the love-soldier.

"Will you shut the fuck up and listen to me?" Ferl's cheeks were flushed in anger, and his hand was on the hilt of his sword. A man could only be interrupted so many times. Several dozen other hands, though, also rested on hilts of daggers or swords. Even plates were being brandished as weapons. Perhaps these men had a modicum of fighting spirit left, after all.

"Now, as I was saying..." His typical eloquence was going to be lost on these men, he realized. "I'm recruiting for a mercenary force. Ferl's Company, eight hundred strong. We're marching on the Oshwon, who have invaded Jecusta unprovoked. I can pay, and experienced soldiers would be welcome. Again, I say I can pay."

Hands moved away from weapons and silence permeated the room. Ferl saw actual consideration in the eyes of many. Some men were probably reliving their so-called glory days, thinking of the comradery of soldiery. Thinking about the thrill of victory. And forgetting about the lice, the crotch rot, and the shit-food. Fingers twitched on weapons, recalling rusty training and maybe assuming that their bodies still had the power to kill, and that their minds had the will. Ferl might dig up a few dusty corpses from this visit after all.

Prickly Beard lowered himself to his stool with an audible creek. "Don't you think we ain't thought about this, boy."

"*Captain* is my title, assuming you choose to serve in my force," Ferl said with a touch of haughtiness. "I don't stand on much formality, but I do insist on respect of the ranks."

"Fine, *Captain*. But, unless yer blind, you can see. We're old. Fat. Hurt. Tired. Not much good fer marching. Not much good fer fighting." Others nodded their assent, and the man who'd revealed his nipple patted his ample belly, though the stump of a leg would have to be a worse hindrance to him.

"Every army needs its officers. What I need is discipline. Experience," said Ferl, smacking one hand into his other to emphasize his words.

Prickly Beard considered Ferl, and Ferl saw that the rest of the veterans were looking to him for guidance. Prickly Beard noticed and stomped his meaty paw on a table, causing a crock to tumble and shatter on the sticky floor. "I ain't yer sergeant no more!" he proclaimed over the room.

"Make yer own decisions with yer lives! I'll not stop any men from marching with you, so long as ya march with purpose. We've had too many bad leaders. People with no caring. People with no values. Tell us, *Captain*. What do ya fight for?"

What *did* Ferl fight for?

He fought because people needed to die.

"My grandfather was killed by the Oshwon in his home. Sampson Nerial was his name; he served and led in the Fifth Division. Murdered in a raid. I fight because I want revenge." Ferl's face had twisted as he spoke, conveying his rage and dedication to the mission.

"Revenge is a good motive, but not the best. A man with vengeance in his brain is apt to make mistakes. He's apt to do anything to see that the blood toll is paid. Is that yer story?" Prickly Beard asked with the typical philosophizing of a long-time soldier.

"I've no wish to die or see my allies killed. I do right by people who follow me, both in pay and treatment. In case you can read, I'm leaving the contracts here with the details. My army is three miles southeast of here, by the Erie Crossroads. We march south in four days; furnish your own weapons if you want better quality. Otherwise, I'll give you the best I can."

The tone of the hall was no longer that of drunken depression. Now, it was tinged with consideration. Ferl knew that he'd won over at least a handful, and he had a strong desire to leave behind the dank stench of the hall. With a nod and a smile, he ducked back out into the light of day.

***

"I heard your speech." An Alganian man—evident from his near jet-black hair and prominent nose—approached Ferl. The man had the bearing of a fighter, and though his clothes were well-worn, they were fine enough stock. He didn't appear to be either a beggar or a down-on-his-luck veteran.

Ferl sighed and gestured for the man to sit on the rough stone bench across from his own. He was making an attempt at relaxation in what passed for a park in Fort Aurabourne, somewhere in between the fort proper and that shit-heap of a veteran's hall. This recruiting business was exhausting work, and he needed to clear his head before his dinner date. But, ever the opportunist, he turned his attention to his visitor with his mind already working on how this encounter could benefit his new venture.

Despite the reek of *kerena*, the bearded Alganian had sharp eyes. He accepted the invitation and sat down across from Ferl. His face was not familiar; Ferl hadn't noticed him in the veterans hall, but the place had been dark and he wouldn't have seen the faces of many of its patrons. It would be surprising, though, to find that a possible Alganian veteran would have been mixing with a bunch of Jecustan ex-soldiers. And Ferl said as much.

"Ah, you'll find that soldiers hold fewer grudges than you'd think. Though they all line up on opposite sides of a field, they fight for the same reasons. Those reasons being that they were ordered to do so. But, the fact of the matter is... I was never a soldier. Just an acquaintance of one of the fat old bastards in there. Name's

Christoph."

"Ferl Nerial."

"Nerial. That name caught their attention. Some of the men seemed to recognize the name of your grandfather. Your story about him true? Killed by the Oshwon? You wanting revenge?" He pulled out a cherry pipe, tamping down some loose *kerena* into the barrel. Ferl wrinkled his nose, but Christoph either didn't take the hint or just didn't care.

Ferl nodded, closing his eyes and leaning his head back as the breeze picked up. It almost granted some relief from the heat. "My grandfather was killed, and I do seek revenge."

Cupping his hands against the wind, Christoph worked his flint-lighter—a fairly new innovation—to get the pipe going. It gave off an awful scent of fish oil. Truly a hideous habit.

"Aye, well, I think you've swayed some hearts and minds. I'd expect a few of those old bastards to sign up. I hope that your revenge does not blind you to the fact that you hold the lives of many in your hands. Life is a precious thing, and..."

Ferl, eyes still closed, felt a sudden, heavy impact. He was flung from his bench and landed hard against the ground, feeling a snap in his shoulder. Squinting against the pain, he could see that Christoph was on top of him, and the man was much heavier than he looked. Ferl struggled, trying to reach his dagger where it sat pinned at his waist.

"Get off, you fucker!" he managed.

Christoph acquiesced, roughly shoving himself off of Ferl and drawing his short sword in one smooth motion. Ferl flung his arms up in a defensive posture, but the blow never landed. Instead, there came a clash of steel just above him as Christoph battled with a third person.

Scrambling out of the way, Ferl painfully pulled himself to his feet, grasping his injured shoulder. A woman with short-cropped hair and the muscles of a warrior bashed away at Christoph's guard with a ferocity that belied her gender. She was wielding a hand-axe, a weapon that would typically have been clumsy and a poor match for a sword, but she spun the thing around as if she were a circus juggler.

Christoph, though, was no slouch. His face was stoic and, though he grunted as he batted her weapon away, his eyes betrayed no fear. His was very much a typical Alganian in fencing style, focusing on defense and wearing down the opponent through careful parries, then surprising his opponent with a sudden, ferocious attack.

It was a beautiful dance to watch, Ferl thought, until he suddenly realized that he was only *watching*, still unarmed. He unsheathed his sword, despite the ache in his shoulder, and keyed in on the battle. He pointed his slender sword at the short-haired woman and he realized that his hand was trembling. He took two deep breaths and edged closer to the whirling combatants. Just an inch at a time.

Neither Christoph nor his attacker could find an advantage, and both were breathing heavily. Ferl noticed that the Alganian was bleeding from a cut on his arm which was already soaking his sleeve in blood. Ferl's heart rattled in his chest at the sight. He half wanted to call for the guards, but glancing around, he saw that his attempt at secluded relaxation had been a bit too effective. No one was nearby.

Ferl finally started to close on the attacker with some semblance of a purpose.

The attacker, seeing Ferl closing in, swore loudly. She hacked at Christoph's guard and pivoted, hurling her axe straight for Ferl. Acting completely on instinct, Ferl dropped to the ground and took a mouthful of dust as punishment. It was well worth it, though, as the axe was not embedded in his chest.

Again pushing himself to his feet, he was greeted by the sight of the woman's firm backside as she sprinted away. Christoph was gripping his wounded arm, though his face still wore the same stoic expression it had before. If it hadn't been for the bleeding and the fact that he was out of breath, the Alganian might have been playing a game of cards.

"Mind grabbing my pipe?" the Alganian grunted, nodding to where the pipe had tumbled into the grass nearby. Grabbing the pipe, Ferl tamped down the *kerena* himself and lit the thing before handing it to the fighter. Christoph stopped holding his wound and grasped the pipe with a hand soaked in his own blood.

He sucked in the smoke and held it for an extended moment before blowing it out the side of his mouth with a whooshing sound. He shook his head at Ferl.

"She wanted you dead. Why?" He nodded toward the tree where a throwing dagger stuck out at an odd angle. It was buried at least two inches deep; that would have done some real damage. Especially if it were poisoned. Christoph had saved Ferl's life.

"Frankly, I have no idea what that woman had against me. While I've been known to fuck and run, I don't think I'd have been drunk enough to forget her." He warily took in the surroundings, wondering whether another attacker lurked somewhere in the growing shadows of late afternoon.

Christoph took another puff and sat down heavily.

"I'm no expert on these matters, but I doubt a jilted lover would be such a damn good fighter or hold quite so much of a grudge. I'd wager that was an assassin. Any idea why?"

Ferl rubbed his bruised shoulder and looked away from his Alganian savior. He needed to get back to the safety of his new army.

"I've made a few enemies. Didn't know any of them would want to kill me." A lie.

Christoph grunted in response.

"Well, I might as well get this sown up and get my ass away from you. I don't want to end up in the path of another killer." But Christoph lingered nonetheless. Maybe he was waiting for a 'thank you' or a reward. Ferl's mentor, though, had told him to hold onto his gratitude as if it were the finest gem. A simple 'thank you' could ended up being a debt worth more than a man's life.

Christoph had followed him to this park for a reason. He wanted something. Ferl took a stab and asked, "Want to join my Company?"

Now, Christoph's stoicism broke and he snickered.

"Nefora's tits, you're a bold one. But, aye. I've been looking for a losing cause to join up with, and yours seems just as useless as any. But..." he gestured to his wound, "it'll be command for me. I've little desire to deal with much hand-to-hand these days. And, I'll be needing six months of back-pay for saving your ass here."

Ferl smiled with amusement. He reached out his hand before remembering that Christoph's was covered in blood. The sticky handshake stained his own palm crimson.

"Well, Lieutenant Christoph, welcome to Ferl's Company."

Chapter 7:
Oshwon Valley, Early Summer

C hristoph had made many mistakes in his life; no one was going to dispute that. A few small mistakes and a couple of big old fucking ones the size of oceans. Joining up with Ferl's Company qualified as the latter.

The creak of damp armor, the crunch of underbrush, and the swearing of soldiers almost drowned out the sounds of nature, but didn't quite cover up the omnipresent screaming. The men who'd been taken in the raid only hours before were already filling the air with their howls as the Oshwon had their fun. Christoph tried to ignore the sounds, locking away his feelings in the steel chest of his mind, but he still found himself shivering periodically.

He was not a fearful man and he was certainly a realist. He'd done some bad things in his life, and he'd expected to do more bad things, having joined up with this mercenary company. But, what he'd seen of the tortured... what he'd heard.... His typical iron stomach was a mixing bowl of reflux and regret, balanced with a hefty dose of cramping from the shit food.

"These woods are too damn thick here. Split the men into groups of ten and, for the love of Nefora's asshole, tell them to watch each other's backs," Christoph said quietly to his sergeants. Despite the noise and the fact that the Oshwon likely knew exactly where the mercenaries placed their feet, keeping his voice fairly hushed felt like the right thing to do. The five sergeants, each one dealing with their own internal issues—both digestion-related and mental—nodded and relayed the orders. Trenlo, a Jecustan veteran, lingered for a moment.

"This is a mistake. Did you see that fucking unreal power they used to cut down Rickard and Dice?" the slightly overweight Trenlo asked, limping fairly heavily on one leg. He'd twisted his ankle on a root right when they'd started the march. Or at least that's what he gave as an excuse.

"Just the aftermath." Another event that had tested Christoph's fortitude. The Oshwon *metsikas* who'd attacked Ferl had not been the only ones in the camp. Thankfully, none seemed to have attacked with much vigor or even more soldiers might be dead.

"Giant blades, six feet wide, were flung right at them. Cut right through their swords and then their skulls. How in the fuck can we fight that? This is a fucking mistake!" Fear was etched on Trenlo's face like a death mask. He unknowingly echoed Christoph's own thoughts. But, Christoph was nothing if not a man of his word. For instance, after his smuggler father had killed his mother, Christoph had promised he'd see the older man dead. And, with the bash of a hammer on a sleeping head, he'd fulfilled that promise.

"That's treasonous talk. This is what we signed up for, Trenlo. And like the captain said... once we win this one, ain't no one going to want to fuck with us. We'll get hired to just sit around and defend some town that no one would dare attack because Ferl's Fucking Company is sitting in defense. We get reputation, we get *safe*."

"This isn't fucking war..." Trenlo grunted under his breath, hurriedly looking away from Christoph. And Christoph knew his wasn't a convincing argument, not when hundreds of men were marching to their deaths amidst the tortured screams of their comrades.

In the distance, through a break in the trees, Christoph saw green and yellow lights flash as bright as a lightning bolt. They were immediately followed by an explosive report and a dozen howls of the injured and dying. A great cracking noise came next and Christoph flinched as a tree, probably hundreds of years old, split and fell in the forest, finding its final resting place amidst that of several of Ferl's Company.

He gripped the hilt of his sword with a strong, skilled hand. He'd hoped he'd not have to draw the fucking thing again so soon, but these woods and these Oshwon did not seem to respect rank.

Another explosion.

More death cries.

It was beginning.

***

Iron Arms Horvath scratched dried, crusting blood out of his prickly gray beard. Once, his beard had been brown and as soft as a doe's back. Lynds had snuggled close and said that very thing more than once. Now, with Lynds gone and the passing of years, the hairs on his face had grown as stiff as pricker weeds. He didn't even like touching it, so rough and rigid it had become. But it wouldn't do to have the thing caked in blood; a man needed to have some level of self-respect.

He shouldered his great, bloodied axe and took a minute to breathe. He'd known he was in poor shape, but marching, fighting, and killing really highlighted just how weak he'd become. Sitting around in a veteran's hall and arguing about imagined prowess and years long past was not the same as actually moving around and engaging the muscles.

Horvath had tried to stay sharp—he truly had. He'd practiced with his short sword, mimicking the drills that Sergeant Leany had put him through as a recruit thirty-five years ago. He'd chopped wood, years' worth, for Widow Pan's boarding house in great heaps. He'd even occasionally gotten into scuffles with men who'd either disrespected his veteran comrades or decided that they needed to test their mettle against a real fighting man. At Horvath's size, he'd often gotten challenged by those with deflated egos, men who thought that they'd be able to prove something by hitting the biggest man in the room. As it turned it, all they proved was how hard the biggest man in the room could hit back.

Regardless, all of that incidental preparation had been nothing like swinging a weapon with the fury of the moment and the strength of desperation. Already, after only two small engagements, Horvath was beyond exhausted. His limbs tremored and his hands ached so much that he could barely grip his axe. Sweat stung his tired eyes, and the arrow wound he'd taken in the ass when fighting the Alganians—thought long-healed—ached as if it'd happened yesterday.

His bastard friends still called him Iron Arms, but he'd gotten that nickname long ago. Now, his limbs more resembled weak and frayed ropes. This whole thing'd been a mistake. Why'd he joined up with that brash little bastard, Ferl?

"Sarg, you alright?" Gens asked him, concern etching the man's rough features. Billsly and Panner were doing the same, staring at his blood-covered face.

Right. This is why.

"Ain't my blood, boys. It's gonna take more than a couple o' these scrawny bastards to take me out."

"More 'an a couple are comin'!" hollered Panner in his deep baritone. He'd been a fantastic singer, back when he'd been young.

He was right; leather-clad bodies, covered in muck to blend in with the forest, were separating themselves from the trees and sprinting forward with a howl. Billsly tried to raise his bow, but got a flung spear to the thigh in return. Fucking Billsly—Horvath'd told the old bastard this was no place for bows, but he hadn't listened. He'd never have gotten a clear shot amidst these trees, especially not with his palsy.

An Oshwon warrior closed on Billsly, machete raised for the killing blow. He hadn't seen Horvath, though, partially obscured as he was by a tree. Horvath swung with the force of a grieving friend, cleaving the man's head in twain.

"Ya got fucking brains on me, Sarg!" mumbled Billsly though gritted teeth. He leaned back and laid in the leaves, the spear in his thigh sticking straight up like a beacon.

"Lazy bastard. Don't you dare go to sleep on me! I'll make a turniquet... ah fuck!"

Another wave of attackers was coming—at least a couple dozen. Horvath hurriedly took in his little force, the remnants of Veterans Hall One Hundred and Twenty Six in Aurabourne. They were depleted, half of them injured or dying, the other half barely on their feet. The fucking Ferl's Company regulars at their flanks had all but collapsed or fled. They were worse than shit on the bottom of a shoe.

Again looking to Billsly, whose eyes were closed tightly in pain, Horvath roared and rushed forward to meet his attackers. He hacked through the guard of the first one, leaving a gaping, glistening cut across his neck and chest. His axe sliced through the wrist of the second, the severed hand flopping into the leaves as the man howled and dove after it. A third Oshwon took a look at Horvath—beard again caked in blood— and turned tail.

More were coming, but for a moment, Iron Arms didn't care. For a moment, his arms felt strong again, like the metal for which they were named. For a moment, the old aches disappeared. For a moment, so did all of the old doubts and regrets, the memories of Lynds. It was all gone as he whipped his head around, looking for more blood.

Iron Arms was roaring as something knocked into his side, throwing him off balance. Horvath pivoted, his axe poised to strike at the next fool who'd come within range.

But, it wasn't another Oshwon. It was a fallen Jecustan, older and with a nose like a cucumber. Iron Arms shook his head, trying to clear away the battle fog and squinting more closely at the face, his brain almost numb from what he was seeing. It was Panner. Old, ugly-faced Panner. They'd used to get ass-falling drunk on the Campaigner's Friend and then talk about lost love. Panner was bleeding from a wicked gash in his neck.

Horvath, suddenly feeling quite weak, batted at Panner's killer with his stone-heavy axe. The Oshwon attackers sidestepped. He tried again, this blow even slower, and received a deep gash on his wrist in return. He didn't lose his grip until the next blow connected solidly with the haft of his axe. Something sharp struck him from behind, and Horvath fell to the earth on lifeless legs.

He lay inches away from Panner's ugly face, his longtime friend appearing anguished in death.

That bastard had pushed the hardest for them

all to march with Ferl.

Horvath was weeping as the machetes came down.

***

Awral held his belly in a vain attempt to keep his insides where they belonged, but his intestines were spilling out nonetheless. His opponent, a skinny Oshwon, was impaled on Awral's cheap spear, gripping the staff of the weapon with frozen hands. The two ended up falling in a heap of blood and bowels—a final, awful embrace.

Rennid had no time to dwell on the loss of his acquaintance, however, as two Oshwon stepped toward him, each wielding machete swords that were in equal parts used for hacking away undergrowth and human limbs. Defensively, Rennid jabbed with his spear to keep them at a distance. He'd purloined a better weapon from a slumbering criminal, but a decent weapon didn't make him a decent fighter.

On either side of him, his slave-soldiers were similarly pressed. The Oshwon didn't fight in ranks, like Ferl's Company attempted to amidst the thick forest. Rather, they embraced the woods by rushing and retreating. They killed and they ran, giving up ground little by little but leaving many more mercenary bodies behind than they left of their own.

Rennid was stepping backwards, still managing to keep his distance, when he went down on one knee, slipping in some bit of guts that had leaked from the pile that had been Awral.

His two opponents, both looking grim, closed

for the kill. Rennid had always been a fighter, if not in skill then in spirit, and he prepared to launch himself at one of the Oshwon. He'd be damned if he went down without taking one of these bastards with him. And, by Pandemonium's spiky gates, maybe he'd get both.

And then Rennid was on the ground, completely blinded and flailing his arms in an effort to figure out what had happened. The after-image, green and orange flashing, filled his vision so much that he thought he'd died or had his head cut off. But, his body was whole, and he'd managed to find his spear as he crawled around.

He was kneeling in something warm and wet.

He grasped his spear protectively with two hands while his vision cleared. His attackers, moments ago hale and hearty Oshwon warriors, were both laying on the group and decapitated, spurting blood in rhythmic fashion. It was pooling around Rennid's own knees.

Rennid's stomach twisted like a dirty dish rag being rung out and he heaved the remains of a horrid meal into the gore surrounding him. When he was done, he looked up and saw a string of dead Oshwon mixed with a much greater number of slave-soldiers. Most had been killed conventionally, but others had been taken by whatever power had decapitated his attackers.

He still knelt, stunned beyond the ability to react, when the woman walked by, her bare feet leaving prints in the bloody muck. A black, ashy mist followed her like a specter.

Ashland frowned as she considered the dead.

***

She hated it, this killing. But Ashland knew

that people tended to hate the things they were best at. The blacksmith eventually resented his hammer. The fisherman would rather toss his pole in the lake at times. The innkeeper would, by some point, just as soon burn down his livelihood, turning the place into kindling. And, in similar fashion, she wished that she did not have to kill.

But life always had different plans.

"This is pitiful," she muttered, stepping by a shivering Alganian slave-soldier who was knee deep in the blood of two decapitated Oshwon and moving toward their hidden town. The meaningless battled the meaningless, and she dominated both. There was no pleasure in that. No honor, as if that term held any real meaning.

There were few Oshwon left standing after the last assault. As expected, the frontal attack by the slave-soldiers had drawn out the bulk of the Oshwon forces. Ferl had been right, as he always was. And, though there was no pleasure in killing, there *was* pleasure in that man. Ashland smiled despite her depression about this whole venture. Yes, there had always been pleasure in Ferl.

She continued forward through the forest, the few remaining slave-soldiers quavering and falling in at her wake. The place—always humid—smelled like a damp charnel house. The sticks and stones rubbed roughly against her bare feet, but this was something that Ashland was well-used to. Her feet had callouses like leather and, in fact, the mild pain from occasional rough rocks was almost pleasing to her.

Ashland loved the pulsing life of the forest. Certainly, the average person appreciated the beauty of the thousand shades of green. The music of the chirping birds. The mysteriousness of the unknown path. But, being a *metsika* greenie—being able to sense and draw *yenas*—she saw so much more.

Though she'd started to tire, she quested simply for the feel of it. Around her, all that was life began to glow in a thousand colors. It was less that the actual world changed in her vision, but rather that her perception dug deeper. The grass and beautiful weeds that were hearty enough to survive in the shadow of the great canopies above had a great concentration of *yenas,* bright in color though small in volume. The trees themselves were more diffuse, but mighty nonetheless, glowing in different colors depending on their stage in the lifecycle. From bright yellow to a deep blue, the lifeforces of the trees filled her world. She reached out to touch a great emerald one, drawing just a figurative ounce of *yenas* to hold within her body.

Most greenies could hold *yenas* for only moments, having to shape it into something before the foreign substance began to tear into their *nerring*, their vessel only being meant to hold their own lifeforce. However, Ashland had always been different; her blood was mixed with sap, as her father would say lovingly. He'd had the power, too. He'd rarely used it, though, and encouraged her to do the same. Perhaps that's why her *nerring* was as callous as the bottom of her feet; she'd always drawn, but rarely shaped.

She could also quest much, much further than the average greenie. Instead of feet, her ability to sense *yenas* stretched great yards. In a barren desert, she could sense a buried cactus from a hundred feet away. That was one of the reasons she'd been brought to Agricorinor as little more than a girl. It was also one of the reasons she'd left that backwards old coffin of a school. Not without harsh words and a harsher escape, however. Her departure had, in fact, been the origin of her new name.

She'd not be welcomed back.

The ounce of *yenas* leant her a modicum of strength, false though it may have been. The tree was young, wild, eager to grow and reach the sun. She felt the same.

Oshwona, the center of this little forest civilization, was growing nearer. She could see an abrupt end to the tree line approaching, with comfortable and well-built wooden houses, painted with bright dye from berries and flowers; it was just in sight. The man-made art did nothing to compare to the loveliness of her questing, but her heart fluttered at the sight of it. There was love in those paintings. Love that she was ready to, or maybe had already, sliced to pieces.

There was nothing for it, though. Ferl had her by the branches, as they said. Well, as she said, anyhow.

Chapter 8:
Fort Aurabourne, Late Spring

A ll in all, a successful if slightly smelly day," said Ferl with a crooked smile, showing just the right amount of teeth. Ashland smiled in return, her own grin appearing a bit more predatory. But that was the way of Ashland; she'd always had a bit of an edge.

Fort Aurabourne's nicest restaurant was... actually nice. The scent of roasted pheasant, garlic, and onions filled the place in a way that made the mouth water, enough even to drown out the fishy smell of the sea and the reek of the streets. The wine was fine and worth paying for, and even the serving people were lovely to look at and represented a diversity of sizes and shapes.

Then, Ferl noticed the violet bracelet on each of their wrists. He frowned slightly, and Violet's den flashed in his mind.

"What's wrong, blue eyes?" Ashland asked, her face twisted in concern. She was too expressive, he always told her. Wore her heart on her sleeve, as they said. A liability in a world like this one, where a stray move could get you killed.

"Stray thoughts is all."

"Stray thoughts from a stray," she said, a smile tickling her lips.

"It makes sense." He smiled in return, but then his face turned more serious. He needed to rip the bandage off and get to the point with her, lest they fall into their old back-and-forth and he lost his nerve. "Remember when we were children, before you left? Playing in the Tan Woods west of the Nerial Estate?"

Ashland smiled wider, a wicked look coming from under batting eyelids. "I wouldn't call us 'children,' given what we did in those woods."

Ferl certainly remembered that particular story.

"You're being coy, my dear. You know exactly the day I'm talking about."

A darkness washed over her expressive face, and it was one that seemed to extend in a radius around her like a dark cloud. She shoved away her wine, spilling the glass onto the floor. The slave-servers scrambled like ants to clean it up, but Ashland paid them no mind. Her deep brown eyes searched his without wavering. "How did you know I was in Fort Aurabourne?"

"It doesn't matter. If I could find you this

easily, what about others? I hear Agricorinor is none-too-pleased with the manner in which you left. And, from what I understand, you are not without other enemies."

Ashland rested her forehead in her hands. "Don't try to manipulate me, blue eyes. I know you too well for that. Just be straight with me. You are recruiting an army and you want me to join. From the stories you told, you aren't going to be winning any battles in the conventional sense, so you need an edge. You need me. I'm not a dimwitted farm girl. I'm a *fucking smart* farm girl. Have you considered just *asking*?"

Ferl had considered just asking, and rejected the idea. He hadn't seen Ashland in nearly six years, not since around when she'd been carted off to Agricorinor by her willing family. She was a successful farmer's daughter; not exactly poor, but a cut below Ferl's level of nobility. They'd been in a fierce argument about her leaving, of course, driven by fear of never seeing each other again. Like a hideous caterpillar, the argument had metamorphosized into a debate over their parents' lack of acceptance of their friendship, and whether their relationship had been a mistake to begin with. Things had turned very bitter at the end, and Ferl had said some awful things.

"I'm sorry, my dear. It's been so long since we've seen each other..."

"Yes, I do recall you saying that you'd rather have your testicles scraped than ever seeing me again."

"...and I was afraid you would remember my last words." He scratched at his chin, the unusual feeling of a blush throwing him off. With impeccable timing, their food happened to arrive just then. Roasted duck for Ferl and a fresh, onion-heavy salad for Ashland. She never ate meat.

The pair sat in a heavy silence while the slave-servers fussed about them, and the unhappy quiet continued into their first few bites.

"Why are you doing this, Ferl? From what I understand, you could live comfortably for the rest of your life without raising a finger. I've lost my pulse on the Eastern Sweeps over the years, but the Nerials would be unlikely to lose all of their wealth. You've plenty of people to exploit, after all. Like my family."

"Is protection the same as exploitation? Do you know how many Nerial lives were lost, over the years, from fighting wars to keep our..." Ferl sighed. This was not a new argument, and treading this path was certainly not going to do him a damn bit of good. "Sorry."

Ashland picked at her salad with her filigreed fork. "Me too." She looked up, hair partially obscuring her eyes. "I've missed you, blue eyes."

"I've missed you, my dear. Can we start over?" Ferl raised one eyebrow, just in the way that she'd used to comment on. "Remember that day in the Tan Woods?" Ferl asked again, more quietly this time. "With Nikolaus and Varian?"

"Fuck, Ferl. You know I remember. The piece of shit bastards nearly killed you." Near unconsciously, Ferl touched the faded scar from where Varian's knife had entered his lower abdomen.

"But they didn't, Sherri. Because you killed

them."

"Do you think I need a godsdamned reminder? We were *never* to speak of this. And my name is fucking Ashland now!" She was shouting now, and the other patrons were glancing in their direction none too subtly. Ferl held out his hands, palms up, as if he were calming a horse. Sherry—Ashland—had always been volatile.

"Ashland... it's okay. I just need to tell you something, the reason I needed to find you. Varian, he is dead. You remember, his neck was severed. But Nikolaus... I learned that Nikolaus survived. A hunter found him and took him to a *metsika* who was gifted in healing. Though he lost a hand and a leg, though he was unconscious for more than a year, he eventually came around. And then his memory began to come back. Nikolaus Linstael, oldest son of the Magnate Willys Linstael, still lives. And he wants us dead."

Ashland paled. "But, I cut him. I cut him so badly! I burned him so badly. I didn't know what I was doing, but we checked! We checked before we ran!"

"Ashland... I checked, but I was bleeding badly after the beating they gave me. My hands were shaking too much. I was bleeding. I didn't *think* I felt a pulse. Running seemed most important." Ferl remembered all the blood. Pools of it. Nearby trees soaked with it. And, it had been mixed with the ashes of the tree that Sherri had drawn from to kill the boys. Ashland. Dammit, he would never get used to that.

It was still a wonder that Nikolaus had survived, but Ferl had grown used to the idea over the last couple of years, since the magnate had announced that his eldest son, Nikolaus, was returning to public life after a brutal attack. Ashland, though, was obviously having trouble processing it. It was that event, the killing, that had sent her down a maze of moral questioning about whether or not her power was evil, whether or not she belonged in society, and so on and so forth.

Frankly, Ferl had tried to be supportive of Ashland's emotional plight following the incident with Nikolaus and Varian. He really had. But all he'd ever had to do was touch the healing wound in his abdomen to know that those boys had needed to be killed. They'd used to fight about that, too, particularly when Ashland would suggest turning herself in for the crime. Was it really a crime to kill pompous murderers?

Ferl looked at his former lover across the table. Ashland's eyes were vacant, her mouth hanging open as she considered all of this. Ferl reached over their dishes to push up on her chin with a single finger in a mock attempt to close her mouth. She grasped his hand with both of hers. They were rough and clammy, but Ferl squeezed them right back.

"What do we do?" she asked in a fearful whisper. Out of all of the magnates, the Linstaels were most known for keeping a coterie of *pasnes alna* in their employ. And given that the *pasnes alna* were not particularly pleased with Ashland, this was a true danger.

"What do you think I've been doing? Gathering an army for my health? It's much harder to kill a man... and a woman... when they are surrounded by a thousand soldiers."

Ashland reached for her wine glass—which had been sneakily replaced by the slave-servers after the spill—and gulped it down without preamble. She stood up unsteadily, shaking her head as if to clear out the bad memories and the could-have-beens.

She glowered down at Ferl. "Fuck you. I'll join your army, but fuck you for telling me all of this, right now, here, in this godsdamned restaurant in this godsdamned asshole of a town. If you would have just asked, I would have, you know. When it's come down to it, though we've fought, though it's been years, I've always been there to help you when you needed it."

Ferl had flinched at each word. "I thought you would want to know why..."

"No, I didn't need to know why. Not now. Not like this. What I've learned, over the years, is that I am an effective killer. Though Varian— apparently not Nikolaus—was my first, there have been many since. It is my doom and my destiny to continue doing this. And when someone you love asks you to do what you do best, you simply say yes. You don't need to be manipulated in a public place."

She started off, her bare feet scraping against the wood of the floors. She glanced over her shoulder one more time, eyes flashing. "And, you blue-eyed bastard. Once we meet at your little camp, you will still be fucking me. Every. Single. Night. You owe me that much from this display."

With that, she pushed aside a slave-servant and slammed open the door, disappearing into the night with a deep, throaty shout of frustration.

Ferl was left staring after her. Ashland was quite the woman, yet fairly unchanged from the girl she'd used to be. She'd confused the Pandemonium out of him then, and that effect had only amplified. He scratched at where her hands had grasped his.

"Um, sir? Would you be able to pay for your fare and leave?" A mousey Jecustan man stood over him, seeming almost afraid to say a word. Two heavies—of the not-slave variety—flanked him. Ferl saw that he had the attention of every other patron in the place. Yes, this reminded him very much of the old Ashland, and he couldn't help but grin ear-to-ear.

The mousey manager stepped backwards alarmingly and the heavies moved forward. Ferl held up his hands appeasingly, chuckling slightly.

"Yes, I will pay. Can you please pack this meal to go? It's about time I was away from Fort Aurabourne. I have business to the south."

Chapter 9:
Oshwon Valley, Early Summer

Ferl climbed over a small mountain of mutilated corpses, and he was pleased.

They'd cut through to the outskirts of Oshwona, and the sounds of battle had faded. There actually hadn't been as much killing as Ferl had expected. Unael's sniffling ambassador, Harivor, had been fairly light on the details, but said that the Oshwon had several hundred fighting men and could muster more if needed. Though many had died on both sides, it didn't seem that Ferl's Company had faced a force nearly as large as predicted. They'd also not faced any more *metsikas*, the reluctant Oshwon mages who'd tried to assassinate him earlier.

So, as they marched into Oshwona, Ferl kept well behind Ashland. Encircled by his bodyguards, his eyes darted back and forth vigilantly in case of some sort of an ambush or surprise attack.

Oshwona itself was clean and tidy. Ferl didn't know what he had expected; the Jecustan nobles pinned these people as savages who were unwilling to allow the lights of civilization to shine into their dank, ignorant forest. Should they have been living in mud and dung huts, piled in random heaps here and there? Or would he have expected them to live in caves, deep in their valley? But, instead, they lived in cozy cabins, situated in neat rows separated by well-maintained dirt roads. The walls were painted with images of nature. Here, a scene of a man bowing before a great serpent, painted in vivid pinks and greens. There, a woman riding upon the back of a great bird. And, down a small alley, he saw the scribblings of a child outlining a family holding hands.

The whole thing was far too humanizing. Ferl gritted his teeth against it, reminding himself of the tortured, cockless corpses that were scattered around the Oshwon Valley. Reminding himself that the reason his company was there to begin with was that the Oshwon couldn't leave well-enough alone, and that they did some terrible things in the Jecustan villages they raided. And, he reminded himself that he'd never really cared for children.

Christoph jogged up toward Ferl with his own bodyguard trailing him. It seemed that the pincer forces were beginning to converge. Christoph was caked in blood, mud, and other unspeakable bits of gore.

"Lieutenant, I've told you. Leaders stay to the rear of things. Your mind is more valuable than your sword," Ferl said, gesturing at the bloodstained hilt of his sword. He noted that his lieutenant, so stoic in the month since they've known each other, was clearly rattled.

"Captain, this wasn't exactly a fight that had a fucking rear. They were hiding everywhere—high in trees, under mounds of leaves. Nefora's asshole, some of 'em were pretending to be among the dead and rose up like fucking ghosts!"

"Nonetheless, it seems like you had it well in hand. Tell me, any more magic?"

"Only one. She killed a dozen before we got her. Then, we saw some flashes from the center line, from that wit... from your woman, Ashland." His face was as grim as it was filthy.

"I certainly wouldn't tell *her* she's my woman," Ferl murmured, eyes on the back of Ashland's as she swayed back and forth, flanked by a few nervous slave-soldiers and some of his regulars. "But regardless, I think we can expect something else, something involving magic. Let's be ready."

"No shit," muttered Christoph, not looking at his captain.

"Christoph, it will be worth it when this is over."

"For who?" The Alganian lieutenant strode off without a glance back, heading down a side street to meet back up with his command. Ferl had flinched at his last words.

Abruptly, Ashland and her vanguard halted. There was some muttering—the familiar sounds of sudden discontent—followed by a few cries of outrage. Ferl leaned on one of his soldiers and stood on the tips of his toes to see what the commotion was.

An Oshwon woman—a matriarch covered in wrinkled tattoos of turtles, of all things—blocked their path. She leaned heavily on a gnarled cane as if she'd barely the energy to stand upright. This Turtle Woman, in and of herself, was not particularly impressive, nor worth halting a march. Rather, it was the sight behind her that was the source of pause and outrage.

A half dozen of his soldiers, each one of them having been taken during the earlier raid, were in living Pandemonium just behind her. From a rough, low scaffolding, each naked man hung strappado, wrists tied behind their backs and shoulders unnaturally dislocated by the weight of their own bodies. All were bleeding from serious leg wounds—deep gashes, missing toes, and so on —and their blood was pooling on the ground.

The worst of it was the pigs. The hairy, jet-black, sharp-toothed pigs who were being bathed in blood and oinking happily at the warm feel of it. Periodically, one would rear up and bite a chunk out of one of the soldiers' feet or legs. As Ferl watched, one nipped off the big toe of an old Jecustan who wailed through his gag and flailed to no avail. The pig rolled onto his back and enjoyed his treat.

"Turn back," said the Turtle Woman in near perfect Jecustan. Though she was stricken with age, her voice rang as clear as a clarion horn, filling the street with its power. No one responded, and the soldiers glanced around, murmuring uncertainly. Even Ashland stepped back, turning her head and meeting Ferl's eyes.

"Ah, fuck," Ferl muttered, pushing through his bodyguards and moving to the forefront. His hand brushed Ashland's arm as he passed, giving her a reassuring squeeze. She practically growled at him.

"Are you all scared of an old lady?" he demanded. From her clear, unwavering eyes, the woman was certainly not scared of them. Her gaze made Ferl's bowels twist like a sailor's knot. Nonetheless, confidence was ninety percent body language, and maybe eight percent pretend. He stood half-cocked, hands on his hips.

"Call off your pigs and release our men. Then, bring your fighters out of hiding, have them lay down their arms, and we'll call this thing off."

The Turtle Woman shook her head, her face as grim as death.

"What is the name of our murderer?" she asked, pointing a bony finger at Ferl's chest.

"Call off your fucking pigs," Ferl said through gritted teeth as he watched a man lose a chunk of calf to the sharp porcine teeth.

"Your name, boy." Her voice was cold and welcomed no argument.

"I am Ferl. And you are dead, if you do not stop those fucking pigs." His forehead was sweating, and he felt a mosquito bite into the back of his neck. He dared not shift, though. This whole thing stank of a trap, and he had to bring his men courage. But he flinched inwardly with every whimper of the hanging men.

"Ferl. Well, congratulations, Ferl. You have nearly doomed an entire people. A people whose history stretches back beyond that of your Jecusta. Back beyond that of even your false gods. Was it so much to bear that we wanted to live a life separate from that which you think is ideal? Was it so damaging to your ego that you needed to come here to subjugate us for the sake of progress? Is the penis of your king so small?"

"I don't need your proselytizing, woman, and I certainly cannot speak to the size of Lord Unael's penis. However, this all started because *your* storied people refused to stay in your godsdamned forsaken valley. Because you had to burn a couple of villages, killing a couple hundred people. A couple of them had the misfortune of being nobles, which means that you made some powerful enemies. But, frankly, I don't care about the reasoning behind any of this shit. We are being paid to neutralize the threat to Jecusta. And you people are a threat. So.... Call. Off. Your. Fucking. Pigs." Ferl had virtually spat the last word, his lips curling back with disgust. This was getting to him, and he did not shift his gaze away from the woman lest he meet the eyes of the tortured.

The Turtle Woman raised a graying eyebrow, creasing her forehead into a web of wrinkles.

"Is that what you believe? That we left our valley and did you some harm? My people *do not* leave their valley. This place is sacred to us. Of those living, only I and six others have left the valley and seen the evils that you people force upon the world. How you make mendants of your farmers—the bringers of life. How you build houses and forts and castles with ridiculous proportions to make yourselves feel powerful. How you say your people have *values* and follow the precepts of your Yetra—of peace and love—and yet let a mother starve while she tries to feed her children. Or start a war and kill hundreds over something as trivial as another few miles of farmland and a scenic lake. Everyone is a slave of someone else."

The Turtle Woman gestured grandly, taking in her meager village and the surrounding, wild valley. A soldier whimpered behind her as he soiled himself.

"In this valley, *we* at least can be free. We can live our lives, simple though you may think they are, in whatever way we wish. We can hunt and fish and farm. We can build and destroy as we see fit. My people can be loners or warriors or poets and no one will stop them. We support each other without ruling each other. We, unlike all of you, are free. You are prisoners, and we care nothing for the lives outside of our valley. We did not leave our valley and do you harm. We never burned any village. That is not our way."

Ferl just growled. "If you truly believe that, maybe you should have sent me a negotiator or ambassador, then, instead of attacking in the night and torturing us to death."

"Let's say you had a home, Ferl—which I doubt, given the look of you. And I walked in with a dozen armed foreigners, all battle-hardened and lusting for blood." That part did not describe his company, but he appreciated the compliment. "Would you walk out, hands spread, and ask what we were doing there? Or would you do everything in your power to get us out of your house?"

Ferl shook his head at the twisted logic of it all; he had to look away. A soldier next to Ashland turned away and vomited, and Ferl could hear sobbing just behind him. Ashland herself watched the tortured closely, refusing to look away from the terror, although tears streamed from her eyes and ran down her delicate cheeks.

"STOP THOSE FUCKING PIGS!" Ferl shouted, his lips pulled back.

She had broken him so easily. Something so many had tried to do in his short life. Why in the fuck did he care about this disposable lot of criminal bastards? They were a means to an end.

Ferl was about to call a for charge, trap be damned, but the Turtle Woman whistled out a shrill sound that cut through the valley like the screech of a hawk. The pigs—all four of them—reluctantly pulled themselves away from their bloody treats and waddled to her side. They pushed against her legs, vying for attention and almost knocking her off of her feet. She ended up kneeling, letting them lick her face with bloodied tongues.

Ferl eyed her warily, and checked on his own men. They were a shambles, edging backwards, nearly every one covered in tears or vomit. They appeared more broken than a hundred dishes chucked down the stairs. There was no courage left here. He needed Ashland to do... something.

But, there was no vegetation around. Nothing for her to draw from; the dirt streets were so tightly-packed and well-trodden that not even a dandelion burst through. And she appeared no better off than the rest of them.

The Turtle Woman glared up from her pigs. "Take your soldiers. Take these men and leave here. They might yet survive their wounds, and we will not pursue you. You will never come back, and tell your king that we will never leave our valley. It will take generations for us to recover, anyhow, if we ever manage. Not many choose to have children, these days."

Her eyes grew hard as she gripped her cane. "If you do not leave, oh... you will probably decimate us. We will be a lost people, wiped from your history books and your libraries and your universities. But, *you* will pay the price in blood. Recall those who came for you last night? There are more of them, and they will cut a swathe through you with their power. Our lost streets will run red with your blood, and your soldiers will break their ankles as they trip over the decapitated heads of the fallen. When all is said and done, my friends, my pigs will gorge themselves on your remains. The few survivors you might have will lack the strength or will to bury their own. And you, Ferl... you—"

"She's bluffing," Ashland spat, her voice hoarse and vicious, interrupting the Turtle Woman.

"What?" hissed Ferl, realizing that his heart was rattling in his chest while his breath came in gasps. He wanted to run. He wanted to flee. He wanted to take this Turtle Woman up on her offer, save these men, and lose himself in the world beyond Jecusta. Certainly, none of his stupid plans or machinations were worth all of this. This was a godsdamned mistake.

"She's bluffing. We've broken their will."

"No, they've broken ours," mumbled one of Ferl's bodyguards. Aron was his name, and he was a veteran of three wars. And, he was backing away, eyes fixed on the Turtle Woman with his face betraying the certainty of their demise.

Ashland shook her head rapidly, her wild, dark hair batting tears off of her face. "They do not want to use their magic. They don't. Ferl, it is a form of addiction. Once a person draws, it is almost impossible to stop. And what is addiction except for a form of imprisonment? These people want freedom."

Ferl gripped the hilt of his sword, observing the Turtle Lady. She was now all but ignoring his company, scratching the chin of one of her pigs with one hand while still gripping her cane with the other. But, looking closely, Ferl could see that her hands shook. Not with age or effort, but with actual fear. She was not as brave as her voice conveyed, and Ashland's words seemed to have hit a nerve.

Clearing his throat, Ferl found that the Oshwon woman's fear brought him strength. "You are bluffing, lady of the Oshwon. You've not the heart for this. You've not the heart to push your people to imprison themselves through becoming addicted to magic. If they do so, they might win while losing their identities. At the very least, if you surrender, they can keep their wills and their values if not their corporeal freedom."

Creaking audibly, even over the moans of the bleeding men behind her, the Turtle Woman rose to her feet. She tossed her cane aside, each of her hands coming to rest gently on the head of a pig. "You underestimate me, Ferl. Our independence means everything to us, and I am willing to do anything to preserve it. We Oshwon are more than you know."

Her eyes seemed to glow red, though it may have just been a subtle trick of the light or Ferl's imagination. One of the pigs slumped to the ground, laying heavily on its side and gasping for air. Then, the other did the same with a heavy sigh.

Without thinking, Ferl threw himself to the ground, clenching his eyes shut and covering his neck with his hands.

Heat—a terrible, blistering heat—consumed him. He might as well have been naked and lying in the midday desert sun of Sestria. The metal buckles at his waist and his thin, iron neck chain were superheated and seared into his skin. He clenched his teeth against the pain, the tears that squeezed out of his eyes turning instantly to steam. Even his sweat melted away. It was as if he had stumbled into an oven.

All around him, Ferl could hear the sounds of death. Shrieks of the burned and the gurgling moans of the dying. He smelled burning meat and leather, and only hoped desperately that none of those smells were his own body. He couldn't tell, so great was the heat.

Abruptly, there was near-silence and, though the heat did not immediately fade, the air lost that suffocating fieriness. Ferl dared to stir and open his eyes.

Ashland knelt next to him, hand on his

shoulder. Her hair was a little singed, but she seemed otherwise untouched. Ferl felt a wave of relief at seeing her well, and then a bowel-twisting guilt for the fact that he'd only tended to his own safety when the Turtle Lady had struck. The Turtle Lady!

She lay face down in the street amongst the two drained and fallen pigs. The remaining animals were keening and crying over her body, their voices nearly human in their grief.

All around Ferl and Ashland was devastation. Aron, his bodyguard, had been prophetic; his fallen body was charred and melted, only recognizable from his discarded double-bladed axe. Behind him, for the next thirty paces, the picture was the same. Bodies, burned and blackened. Some writhed with the agony of their burns and a few even attempted to struggle to their feet. The stench of it brought bile to the base of Ferl's throat while the guilt of it clenched his jaw so much that he thought his teeth might break. Those who'd been spared were too stunned to move.

And yet, the paradox was that a bit of joy bubbled up in him to realize that it was his soldiers who were dead rather than him. Thankfully, he'd survived. Just as he always had.

"How?" asked Ferl, trying to catch Ashland's eyes with his own as he pulled himself up. She wouldn't meet his gaze, but instead stared at her own feet.

"I was holding a little extra *yenas*. Not enough to help our men, but enough to keep us safe.... You and me," she mumbled. He touched her chin with a delicate finger. She batted it away as if he'd attacked her, and she bared her teeth like a wolf. "Enough of this! I've had enough of this, Ferl! This was a mistake!"

"Fuck, Ashland." Ferl drew his sword and began to walk toward the tortured men. "You think you need to tell me this was a mistake? This whole venture of mine has been a mistake. I'm a Yetra-fucked fool."

He kicked one of the fallen pigs as he passed. A live one lunged at him and he drove his sword straight through the thing's neck. It didn't die immediately, instead falling to the ground and writhing around in its own blood. The howl was awful, and still far too fucking human.

He approached the scaffolding and reached up to his full height. He hacked at the ropes of the first man. Once, twice, three times. The soldier landed hard in the blood, muck, and excrement, his arms twisted unnaturally behind him. He'd probably never fight again. Likely enough, he'd be lucky to be able to wipe his ass without help.

Ferl turned back to Ashland, shouting his words. "But, fool or not... mistake or not... we are finishing this thing! We are finishing this, Ashland!" He reached up and freed another soldier before realizing this one had already died of blood loss. Ferl sighed and blinked away a stupid, stray tear. And then he batted away one of the hundreds of flies that had begun to congregate.

A handful of his men, far enough behind the front lines to have survived the blast, were picking their way through the blood and the gore, moving to help their captain in cutting down the bodies. The looks he received would have killed a lesser man, but they all skirted Ashland so widely that he knew no one would dare strike.

In the distance, he could see some of his men slowly retreating back toward the forest and the valley. Deserters that he frankly couldn't blame for their cowardice. But he'd have to punish them nonetheless, just like he had Dammey.

Ferl still spoke to Ashland, but so that all of the rest of the men could hear him. "These Oshwon have nothing left. This was their final trap, sprung right in our faces. But we weathered it, and, after today, our lives will be much easier. Just a final push..."

Ashland turned her head away from Ferl's. Her fists were clenched, and Ferl wondered whether she might join the deserters. But she stood firm, if somewhat unsteadily. Her posture bespoke her anger. She was not convinced by his honeyed tongue; she knew he feared, and she knew he put on a show for his men.

"What in the name of Nefora's tits is this?"

Christoph and his guard approached the scaffolding from the other side, witnessing the bloody aftermath with heavy, reddened eyes. He was puffing from his pipe and his hands were shaking like an old man's. He shook his head wearily, trying to take in all of the devastation.

Ferl went to meet his lieutenant, gathering himself. "This was their trap. It sprung, but we survived. Your men are intact, I take it?" Christoph's eyes were fixed on the slow dying pig that Ferl had pierced. The lieutenant was lost in the spell of its rhythmic flopping.

"Christoph!" Ferl's sharp voice cut through

the stupor. Christoph blinked and squinted at him.

"Yes, Captain. No resistance. In fact... you will need to come and see this. I think... I think we've won."

"Perfect. Lead the way."

***

The square at the center of Oshwona was full of carvings.

There was no artistic theme here. To Ferl's left was a poorly-carved bull that was only recognizable by the very real horns that protruded from its rough, blocky head. To his right were three women—very detailed ones— making love to a corpulent man. Ferl raised an eyebrow at the unrealistically large member that the carved man gripped with his paw of a hand. Yet, he didn't spend much time looking at any one carving; there was a forest of them, and he was well-distracted by the hundreds of Oshwon grouped together in the middle of this mess.

There were men, women, and an abundance of children sitting in small groups together, quietly conversing in whatever language it was that they spoke. None held any weapons, though many men—strong ones—were among this group and could well have been bringing them a fight. A number wore tattoos just like those of the Turtle Lady and those men who'd attacked them earlier. They seemed to be pointedly *not* paying attention to the ragged, bloodied soldiers who were slowly closing into a ring around them.

It was a fairly small ring. Ferl's slave-soldiers had nearly been entirely lost in the frontal assault. He saw Rennid, the short Alganian slave-sergeant, using his spear to compensate for a leg wound. Only about half of the veterans of the One Hundred and Twenty Sixth seemed to be present and coming from the south. The prickly bearded Iron Arms—their reluctant, de facto leader—was nowhere to be seen. His criminals and misfits, who had been positioned behind the slaves and from a northern assault, were worse for the wear, but still somewhat numerous. Doing some quick calculations, Ferl estimated that he'd lost just over half of his forces.

And, even now, he suspected one final trick.

Ashland strode in next to him, pointedly ignoring his gaze. The set of her jaw revealed just how angry she was at him—just not so angry that she'd let him be killed. Her legs were quaking, though, and Ferl wondered exactly how much energy she had left. He'd himself fought nothing but a pig, and he felt like he could lay down in the dirt for a solid two days.

Ferl cleared his throat. "Who among you is in charge?" No one responded.

"Okay. Who speaks for you, then?" That got a reaction. An Oshwon man—bare of tattoos and with his shirtless body beginning to sag with age —stood up from a small group of children where he'd been animatedly telling a story.

"I am Charma. I speak for these free peoples. Today, at least," he said in a halting accent. He lacked the precise control that the Turtle Woman had had, but his voice certainly held a dose of vitriol which showed that he understood everything that was happening.

"Then you can tell these people that they have lost. That, for their transgressions, they must leave this valley, never to return. Tell them that my men will put this town to torch, and advise them that returning, or inflicting any violence or committing any crime in Jecusta, will lead to their deaths."

Charma gritted his teeth and balled a fist, but made no move to attack. He gestured in the direction Ferl had come from, back toward the scaffolding.

"Aletah said that, if we were to see the flash of her power, it would be over. That any more fighting would be futile and only result in further death and the possible extinction of our peoples. Tell me, marauder, is Aletah dead?"

"I am not a marauder. I have been hired by the lord of Farrow's Hold to put an end to your aggression. But, if you are referring to the turtle-painted woman who was torturing my men with her pet pigs? Yes, last I saw, her remaining pig was feasting on her face."

Charma's cheeks flushed in a rage. Ferl almost wanted him to rush forward; Ashland would make short work of him. But, then he saw all of the children watching their conversation sidelong, and he realized that this couldn't end in violence.

All at once, Charma deflated. "She was a great woman, Aletah was. A great guide and a great mother.... We respect her opinion, but we make our own choices. Today, they align. Our people will leave this place. Preservation is more important than retention of our ancestral lands. Our people have never been nomads, but certainly we can carve out a land for ourselves. However..."

Charma looked up, his eyes fiery with intensity. "If you burn our home and this grove, this sacred place, you will have to make corpses of us all. And we will continue to fight you. Even our children will come to you with sticks, rocks, and fists. This grove is our heritage and our history. Our home has done you no harm, and our carvings and art are a wonder. Are you such a monster that you will allow that to come to pass?"

Ferl shook his head, the sight of Aletah's torture still in the forefront of his mind. "Monster is a relative term. I remind you of the pigs. My lords were very clear—this place is to be wiped away so that you may never return. It is not to be colonized, and your forest will be used for lumber in an effort to rebuild the villages you destroyed."

Charma pulled a spear from behind a carving, one of a snake the size of a horse. Others nearby rose to their feet, finding their own rough weapons. Some with tattoos held animals or had their hands pressed against the ground. More *metsikas*. Weak, maybe, but enough of them to do some damage.

"Then this will be the end of it," said Charma, his voice sorrowful, but with no bow in his back.

Ferl's own men, spread throughout the carving grove, exhaustedly readied their own weapons. That they would win, there was no doubt. There were few warriors among the Oshwon, and those who were there would be preoccupied with protecting the children. Even the *metsikas*, though they could do some harm, were reluctant to fight and would undoubtedly hold back.

Ashland dug her nails into Ferl's hand, almost deep enough to draw blood.

"No more!" she hissed. "End this. No more bloodshed."

She was right. This needed to end. He'd no heart to kill children. And, though this Charma irritated him, and despite Aletah having tortured his men in an inhumane, monstrous way, he had little desire to kill those who could not fight back.

Plus, getting out of this valley with no army left intact would render this entire venture useless. And Ferl was not about to accept that failure.

"Everyone, put down your weapons. Down!" Ferl waved his arms like a father directing aberrant children. "I've little leeway to disobey my lords. Typically, if they say 'burn it down,' I make fire. However, perhaps we can come to another arrangement."

Ferl's mind raced; how could he appease the Jecustan nobles—who were out for blood—while fulfilling the terms of this contract *without* killing the rest of these people? Ferl thought of Lord Unael and his struggles with wrangling the nobles. He thought of the economy, somewhat suppressed since the last of the true wars twenty years before. He considered his last visit to Farrow's Hold, where age, decay, and thoughtlessness had begun to infect the foundations of the city—at least as the older nobles saw it.

He realized he needed to say something; all eyes were on him. With that realization, the blood pumped through his veins, adrenaline bringing some life to his limbs and some energy to his voice. This was what he lived for. To persuade the unpersuadable. To negotiate the impossible deal. To convince others of the ultimate truth. Ferl was always right. Or, at least nearly almost always so.

"I believe I could convince the lords to leave this valley as a monument to your people. For your town and grove to be retaken by the wilds of the forest. Your legacy will be preserved. However, your freedom will not be. Your people will need to come back with me, to Farrow's Hold, and agree to serve the lords of that place. You will need to leave your roots behind in this place, and I will do everything in my power to ensure this place be spared. Celebrated, even, as a landmark."

Charma glared at him, debating whether or not to call on his people to attack. Then, abruptly, he let his spear fall to the earth. It wasn't that the fight went out of him; it was that he was sending a signal to his people that said "not yet." This man—and these Oshwon—would be extremely dangerous to transport to Farrow's Hold. Since they had no real leader, any one of them might operate his or her independence and slit one of their throats on the way back.

Ferl just hoped that the symbolism of freedom outweighed the actual need. These people seemed to put a lot of stock into their charms and symbols. Saving this so-called sacred grove and its carvings of bulls and giant penises could truly motivate them to serve, he thought.

"I agree to your terms." Charma spat phlegm into the dirt. "My people are welcome to make whatever decision they'd like." He turned and chanted something in the language of the Oshwon. There was a long pause... the type that might act as a precursor to a hurricane. But, after a minute, an elderly woman tossed aside her kitchen knife and spat into the ground.

A chorus of similar responses filled the air as hundreds also spat. A strange custom, but one that Ferl expected meant reluctant acceptance. Nonetheless, this was not yet a done deal. The nobles would be much happier if he transported back a prize that could be controlled.

Ferl scanned his soldiers. He picked out the stocky, ragged Alganian, his slave-sergeant. "Rennid, to me."

The slave-sergeant limped over cautiously, but kept his eyes carefully lowered. The perfect mix of assertiveness and subservience. "Captain?"

"Rennid, as promised, your people are free." Ferl cleared his throat. "Those of you who remain. You are to have the permanent cure, and I hope that you will stay as part of my company as fully-paid mercenaries."

The freed slave only nodded blankly. Ferl wasn't sure what he himself had expected; maybe a grin or some sort of jovial reaction. Maybe recognition that Ferl had actually kept his bargain. Maybe something to indicate that Ferl was not the monster that the Oshwon believed him to be.

Though, he was about to be a monster.

"Now, Sergeant Rennid... if you still be in my service, I have my first true order for you as a freed man." The Alganian raised his eyes for the first time. Ferl could see the conflict in those orbs

—he was a man suddenly given everything, and without having a clue what to do with it. After a moment, Rennid nodded once, firmly.

"Perfect." Ferl took in the men, women, and children of the Oshwon. He saw rage, uncertainty, and sadness written on their faces. Children clung to mothers or relatives, and fathers stood protectively over their families.

Ferl set his jaw. Ultimately, this would be for their own good. He cleared his throat.

"Rennid, bring me the remainder of the Liquid Collar."

Chapter 10: Epilogue

Tomorrow, they would be at Farrow's Hold. Tomorrow, Ferl's Company would be officially sanctioned as the eleventh legal mercenary company allowed to operate within the bounds of Jecusta. Tomorrow, his company— that which remained—would be paid handsomely, with the money which might have gone to the fallen divvied up among the living.

Tomorrow, this would all be over.

But, tomorrow, it would also truly begin.

"Pass the Campaigner's Friend," said Ferl to Christoph, sitting at a dwindling campfire. Christoph acquiesced, tossing over a flask of the rotgut that had been helping to erase some of the... rougher memories of the Oshwon Valley. Luckily, a couple of the surviving veterans of the One Hundred and Twenty Sixth knew the recipe, and Ferl had had no qualms about dishing out the yets necessary to allow the Campaigner's Friend to flow like water.

Christoph and Ferl had not talked much on the march back. Christoph had been aloof, distant, although his duties in wrangling the Oshwon prisoners had certainly pulled him away. Ferl, himself, had found little reason to fraternize with his soldiers, or even his command staff. Some evenings, he'd force his men together to give a heart rousing speech that was greeted as pleasantly as a fart at a wedding. Then, he'd get back to his heavily-guarded tent. Alone.

Ashland had little to say to him.

He knew that what had happened with the Oshwon sat poorly with his childhood love. Quite accusatorily, she'd interrogated him about the Oshwon contract. Had Unael told the truth? What were Escamilla's motives? What research had he done on the Jecustan nobles' claims regarding the Oshwon invasions? Ashland had believed Aletah, the Turtle Lady, when she'd said that the Oshwon had never left their valley—that the people had in no way invaded Jecustan soil.

Ferl argued that it didn't really matter, that they were just doing their job and what they were being paid for. If they hadn't taken the Oshwon, then another mercenary company would have. The Ironshod, maybe. If that had happened, Ferl and Ashland would have been completely out of luck, without the protection of an army against the many who wanted them dead.

Then, Ashland had called *him* the aggressor. Simple words, but ones that had infuriated him to no end. He had exploded with rage, screaming that it was she who'd enabled them to enslave these people. Overall, it had ended poorly, and they hadn't spoken for several days.

But Ferl needed to talk to Ashland and Christoph tonight in order to discuss short-term next steps and long-term strategy. Ferl had been delaying it, hoping that time would decay the memories of Oshwona for both of them. And it would, he knew. Time always did with soldiers. If the Fort Aurabourne veterans proved anything, it was that soldiers were skilled at twisting the memories of battle into something both false and grand.

"Blue eyes." The words floated into his ears like music.

Ferl felt a tickle as Ashland ran her nails along the back of his neck. She lingered for a second before sitting cross-legged in the grass across from him. He could see her digging her bare feet into the grass and knew she was likely drawing *yenas* for the feel of it. Her features were as serene as he could remember seeing them. Maybe she wasn't holding a grudge.

"Ashland. Thanks for joining us."

"When the captain comes calling, the soldiers come running," she said with no hint of sarcasm. Ferl shook his head and tossed her the flask. Ashland took an unaware sip before coughing and sputtering. Christoph chuckled before catching himself. Ashland made the Alganian fiercely uncomfortable, and he seemed bound and determined to keep it that way.

Ferl cleared his throat. "We are near the gates of Farrow's Hold, and tomorrow, our first impossible contract will have been fulfilled. We've done it, thanks to the both of you."

Ashland scrunched the grass between her toes while Christoph simply puffed away on his *kerena* pipe.

"But we need to think about what is next. We will now have a sanctioned mercenary company, allowed to operate in an official capacity within Jecusta—so long as we are hired by someone with some level of noble blood. This being Jecusta, there are enough of those to drown in. Soon, we are going to be awash in work of a much safer variety," said Ferl. Ultimately, though, he had plans beyond the humdrum of mercenary life.

Christoph set down his pipe and met Ferl's eyes across the fire. He clearly had something he'd been wanting to say, but hadn't quite found the time for it. Ferl nodded and raised his eyebrows.

"Captain, how does it feel?" Christoph asked, his voice quiet.

"How does what feel?"

"The revenge. Your grandfather, killed by the Oshwon. You have your revenge now. That was the reason you gave for this entire venture, no? I've been there before, Captain. I've had my revenge. I want to know—how does it feel for you?"

Ferl considered Christoph. The Alganian was painted with exhaustion, it was true, but his eyes were as sharp as an eagle's. This was a calculated question, and Christoph knew Ferl's lie for what it was. He probably always had. He deserved to know the truth, as did Ashland. In fact, they *had* to know the truth. Ferl sighed deeply.

"I'd already gotten my revenge—not *for* Samson Nerial, but *on* Samson Nerial. My grandfather died by my own hand, months ago. I slit his lying throat and held his hands as he bled out. A fitting end to such a bastard."

Ashland gasped and twisted to her feet. "No, Ferl... you didn't!" Christoph nodded, as if it was what he'd already expected.

"I did, Ashland. You know more than anyone that he deserved it. It just took me some time to do what I needed to do. Granted, it wasn't an ideal execution. He cut me pretty badly beforehand, but I struck last and he knew what he had done wrong when I jammed the dagger into his heart." Ferl's lips twisted in disgust at the memory. Samson was an abusive, fierce old bastard. Well-liked by the military sorts, but commanded his family with fear and pain. It was no wonder the Nerials had mostly fled or died off.

Christoph picked his pipe back up and puffed a ring of smoke. He seemed unaffected by Ferl's reveal. "I've been down that road. Killed my own father because he needed killing. It was emptier than I thought it'd be. Captain, did it help?"

Did it help? An Ultner-fucked question. Probably in the short-term, but there were more people who needed to die. Ferl merely shrugged at his steadfast lieutenant.

Ashland had begun to pace around the fire, gesturing wildly with her arms. "I can't believe he's dead. Samson was not the monster you made him out to be. He was fucking family. All you had."

Ferl spat and stood up himself. "He was exactly the monster I made him out to be. Worse, even! You've no idea the things he did, that he managed to cover up under this guise of nobility and honor. The worst bastards hide it best. But, I saw through it—"

"And managed to make yourself rich in the process!" Ashland hissed.

"That's not what this is about, Sherri! It's far, far more than just fucking money! It's about godsdamned justice!" Ferl's hands were shaking with the anger of it. It wasn't anger at Ashland, though. He'd manipulated her, and she deserved to vent. It was more at the reminder of the injustices, and of the people who still needed to die.

"My name is fucking Ashland now!"

The two faced off, only inches away from each other. Her delicate features were twisted in judgment, as if she had some pedestal to stand on. She'd killed far less deserving people. Ferl felt the urge to grab her, to shove her back onto the ground and force her to listen. She never fucking listened to him. But, if he did that, she'd probably blow him to pieces.

Christoph cleared his throat, breaking the silence and the tension.

"Okay, so why'd you start this company, Captain? No more lies," the Alganian admonished. Ferl shot Ashland one more sharp look, but then he sat back down.

"I didn't precisely lie, Lieutenant. I told you I needed revenge and that people needed to die. I just wasn't talking about my grandfather— anymore—or the Oshwon. They were a means to an end. I needed a sanctioned army to truly mete out justice." Ferl's gaze went inward, focusing on the memories that fueled his venture.

"First, for me *and* Ashland, it is Nikolaus Linstael, heir to the magnatedom of the Eastern Sweeps, who needs to die. For crimes against me and my family." Ashland hurriedly looked away.

"Second, Lissandra the Black. I've no time to tell her story, but know that she needs to die in a hideous fashion. For crimes against me."

"Finally, you've all heard of Eramore, the Wandering Knight? Of course. Everyone has. Well, he wanders no longer. And *he* needs to die most of all. For crimes against my mother. His wife."

ABOUT THE AUTHOR

Mike Sliter was born in the deep wilds of Cleveland, Ohio, where he fought off at least two siblings for scraps of pizza. His bedroom, growing up, was a monument to fantasy, containing a stack of worn and well-read books, a medieval Lego civilization spanning half the room, and a very real sword circa World War II. Today, he pursues his fantastical passion by writing novels to supplement his day job as a leadership consultant.